CAPITOL BREAK

A CHRIS COLLINS CIA THRILLER #1

DAVID BERENS

JOHN HOPTON

TROPICAL
THRILLERS

For those who question everything.

ROGUE ENEMY

A CHRIS COLLINS CIA THRILLER PREQUEL

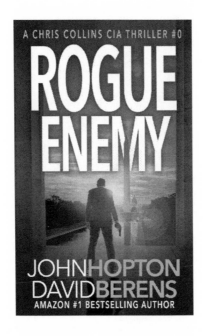

GO BACK TO WHERE IT ALL STARTED
Be sure to grab the FREE prequel to this book called

ROGUE ENEMY - A Chris Collins CIA Thriller
available HERE
and at www.tropicalthrillers.com

GET MORE OF MY BOOKS FREE!

As a thank you for buying this book, I'd like to invite you to join my Beachbum Brigade Reader Group. You can get 4 FREE BOOKS for joining absolutely FREE.

To join, click tropicalthrillers.com/readergroup and your free stuff will be sent immediately. It will never cost you anything, ever!

For more information, visit tropicalthrillers.com

CAPITOL BREAK

A CHRIS COLLINS CIA THRILLER #1

PROFESSIONAL NECESSITY

Chris Collins took a sip of Dom Pérignon champagne and savored its complex, soul-warming flavors. Everything about the event he was attending was as top-notch as the champagne, but the drink was the only thing he was enjoying. As he surveyed the opulent room, his eyes fell on all the things he did not enjoy about events like these. The fake smiles, the transient conversations, and the outfits that straddled the line between looking classy and looking like they'd been pulled from a costume box in a fancy dress shop.

A perfect example of the latter glided towards him, filled by a woman Chris had no genuine connection to but was obliged to talk to out of professional necessity. He was pretty sure her name was Jean and she worked for a think tank. Her electric blue dress looked like something a child would wear if they were pretending to be a princess, and her gold earrings were so large it seemed as if they should be stretching her earlobes.

Just keep walking, Jean, Chris thought to himself. *Kissing me on both cheeks is not going to improve either of our lives.*

Jean came closer.

"Chris!" she said, kissing him on both cheeks. "I must say you're looking as wonderful as ever!"

"Likewise," Chris replied. Technically it wasn't a lie; out of social convention he 'must' also say that, even though he didn't believe it.

"It's a magnificent evening," Jean continued. "How are you enjoying the band? I know you're a man of exceptional taste."

"If I could hear them over the sound of shallow conversations I have no doubt they'd be excellent," Chris said. She laughed, and Chris smiled back to uphold the idea that he was joking.

"I simply love Bach," Jean told him, smacking her lips as if Bach were a taste.

"It's Bassani," Chris advised her as she floated away, onto the next flavorless interaction. He tried to appreciate the sound of a violin that was drifting across the room, but it was lost in the white noise.

The brief respite was interrupted by another person that Chris was expected to be friendly to. Norman Brickdale, an investment banker who was cozy with members of the Cabinet. A man whose immaculately tailored dinner suit was undermined by the distraction of his errant comb-over and the kind of angrily red nose only found on very heavy drinkers.

"Mr. Collins," Norman said, firmly shaking Chris's

hand and laughing for no apparent reason. Norman's wife kissed Chris on both cheeks.

"You're looking as handsome as ever," she said, before briefly casting her eye over the graying hair at his temples. The last few months had seen a major increase in the graying.

"Huge congrats on the new job," Norman said, beaming.

"It was a demotion, but thanks," Chris replied. The couple drifted away without responding.

Chris looked up towards the ceiling, glancing at magnificent chandeliers reflecting the ballroom's gold leaf trims in their crystal droplets. He barely admired the aesthetics as his mind turned to more practical matters.

He had recently been demoted from his position as Deputy Director of the CIA, and was now doing little more than shuffling paperwork. Nobody had asked him to make their coffee yet, but he was effectively doing the kind of admin work generally assigned to someone just starting out in their career.

His name was still on some people's lists of supposedly influential figures to invite to gatherings such as this. Usually, he turned the invitations down. He'd agreed to attend the event tonight, a fundraiser, because he thought he might make some new connections. But even after several glasses of champagne he found his enthusiasm for networking was at rock bottom.

Right now, he was surer than ever that he had to get out of the CIA. He thought about how often his wife had been asking him to get out of the agency that had consumed so much of his life. Their lives. Aside from the fact that she wanted her husband back, there was now another motivation to leave. A recent lawsuit had taken every penny they had ever saved, and the money that had once been his savings was now in the bank account of people who had somehow won an outrageous compensation claim against him.

Leaving the agency to join a private firm, an idea that had been at the forefront of his mind recently, would make financial sense. It would also allow him more time to spend with his wife, and maybe even give him back a little of his dignity.

Chris's thoughts were interrupted when the sound of violins stopped and was replaced by an unpleasant clanging noise emanating from several speakers. Emma Oakland, the chief fundraiser, was tapping her champagne glass half an inch from a microphone.

"Ladies and gentlemen ... ," she said, drawing out her words as if they were of extreme importance. "Please welcome to the stage a man who, after his meteoric rise up the political ranks, needs no introduction. But I'll give him one anyway: Matthew McGoldrick!"

Cheers and applause filled the room, accompanied by whoops of delight coming from some of the female attendees. Senator McGoldrick had recently announced his candidacy for the presidential primaries and had been getting a lot of highly positive media coverage. But the supposedly sophisticated crowd now facing the stage made it sound as if some rockstar heartthrob, or possibly a hunky male stripper, was about to appear.

With a long, confident stride, McGoldrick walked onto the stage, his swept-back blond hair looking like every strand had been put in place by D.C.'s greatest stylists. He flashed a Hollywood smile as he waved at the crowd, occasionally stopping to clasp his hands together in a symbol of love and humility.

"Thank you! Thank you so much," McGoldrick said to his audience. "You're too kind!" Finally, the applause subsided.

"I want to talk to you about how we can build a better world … "

Ambitious start, Chris thought to himself, as McGoldrick's words echoed around the hall. The politician continued to wax lyrical about how love and mutual respect can help to heal the divisions in America, while Chris wrestled with the cynicism that years of trying to make the world a better place—with mixed success—had given him. He also tried to ignore the feeling that McGoldrick was too good to be true. Someone had to try to take the country in the right direction, even if their only plan right now seemed to be clichés and hyperbole.

"Which is why I was so delighted to announce my intention to run in the primaries!" McGoldrick stated to the crowd, who erupted with even greater fervor than they'd disgorged when he entered the stage. Having seen more than enough, Chris turned and walked out of the hall.

AN INCH AWAY

Candlelight flickered in the glass sphere of a lamp sitting on a pristine white tablecloth. At either side of the table were a man and woman, their eyes locked during a moment of silence. They'd shared these quiet gazes back when they first met, when they were lost in each other's affections. Now, affection had been replaced by contempt. Mutual thoughts of *I swear that is the most beautiful person I have ever seen*, had been replaced by *I dare you to say it*.

"Just say what you want to say," the man spoke up.

"How can you have reached this age and still think you're the world's most irresistible man?" the woman asked. "Don't you get bored of your own ego?"

"What makes you think I think that?" the man replied. "I mean, I do think that. But why are you asking me now?"

"The little winks and smiles you're giving the waitress.

Like she can barely concentrate on her work because she can't stop looking at you."

The man grinned, showing gleaming white teeth. Tsu noticed the candlelight dancing on his shiny, swept-back black hair. She'd once thought he was unbelievably handsome, but now his attractiveness just irritated her.

The waitress arrived at the table with two plates of exquisitely presented food, the delicate ingredients built together in the center of the plate and covered with a light flourish of sauce.

"Your wife is very beautiful, sir," the waitress said as she put down the plates. "You are a very lucky man."

"She's not my wife, but yes, she is," the man told the waitress, smiling and looking at her like he was trying to melt her heart. When she walked away, he turned back to Tsu and said:

"That was weird,"

"You don't know why she said that?" Tsu asked him. "She's trying to tell you she doesn't want to be hit on by a man who's having dinner with his ... whatever I am."

"Colleague with benefits?"

"I'm not sure what the benefits are. Whenever I'm with you, I spend the day trying not to get killed and the evening getting wooed by someone who thinks I'm supposed to be impressed by a six-pack."

Tsu and her colleague, Marco, were the only diners in the restaurant, which was far too expensive for most residents of Yangon to even consider. It was the epitome of old-world refinement save for the Burmese pop music playing a little too screechily in the background.

"It's not my fault people try to kill us," Marco said. "That just comes with the job."

Tsu was about to respond when blood exploded from her date's head, the gruesome sight registering just before the sound of the gunshot that caused it.

Tsu saw Marco's eyes roll back before she instinctively ducked under the table, pushing it over in front of her. More bullets hammered into the wall behind her, the ear-splitting sound stopping her from thinking straight. Another bullet crashed into the table an inch from her hand, tearing right through the wood and twisting the metal of the table leg. Then, there was silence.

She peered around the side of the table to see a man dressed in a white muscle vest and black leather motorcycle pants walking quickly out of the restaurant.

Her eyes scanned the cutlery scattered on the floor and she put her hand on a steak knife, still lightly covered in creamy brown sauce. She threw it hard across the room, pointing her arm dead straight after it. It thudded into the assailant's back and he screamed before slumping to the ground. She stood and moved towards him, reaching him as he was getting to his knees.

She yanked the knife from his back to use again, but as she drew back her arm he sunk his teeth deep into the flesh on her leg—flesh that was rarely bare but had been exposed by the evening dress she'd chosen.

She gritted her teeth and growled, pulling her leg away. The man got to his feet and came at her, taking hold of her knife-carrying right arm and gripping it tight. She swung her left hand and her fist connected with his jaw, then she brought it back quickly for a second swing. She felt his jaw break as she landed again, but he didn't let go of her arm and was going for her eyes with his fingers.

She mustered all her strength and swung a third time. The man's grimace turned to a blank expression as he lost consciousness, swaying to his right and towards the ground.

Tsu tucked the knife under her fist and threw a punch with her right hand, keeping the blade away and giving the man a final blow for good measure. He dropped forwards face first, his body completely limp.

She ran over to Marco who was still in his chair, his head resting on his shoulder. She checked him carefully for a pulse but felt nothing. She closed her eyes to compose herself, then she gently closed his.

The waitress emerged cautiously from the back of the restaurant and audibly drew breath when she saw Marco.

"It's okay," Tsu told her, pulling out some notes and putting them on the table. "No police, okay?"

The waitress stared at her, stunned.

"Okay?"

The waitress nodded.

"Sorry you had to see this," Tsu said. Then she walked across the room, picked up the attacker by his hair, put her arm around his chest and carried him out of the restaurant.

～

THIRTY MINUTES later and half a mile across town, the man's eyes opened and he looked down. He saw his own feet, still protected by leather motorcycle boots but bound together tightly with rope. Then he felt heat close to his face. He swiveled his eyes and saw his head was being held an inch from the plate of an electric cooker, the metal ring glowing bright red.

CRYSTALLINE BLUE

Chris pushed open the door to his home and entered his kitchen, the welcoming smell of wine and freshly cooked garlic greeting him as he kicked off his shoes. His wife was sitting at their handsome oak table, a glass of wine in one hand and a book—opened at the title page—in the other.

"Any left for me?" Chris asked Alice.

"Dinner or wine?"

"Well, the last time I checked, we had around twenty bottles laid down. So if there's no wine left, I'm impressed."

"There's plenty of wine left," Alice said, smiling. "But no dinner. I thought you'd eat at the event?"

"The event put me off my food."

Chris sat down and poured himself a glass of Barolo Riserva. One of his many favorite reds.

"Enjoy that," Alice said. "Once we've finished what's in the cellar, we'll have to switch to moonshine."

Chris took a sip of the Italian wine and let it sooth his bones as he forgot everything for a moment. But taking his time over the rest of the glass was impossible, and it was soon gone.

"Or drink it all as quickly as possible, like ripping off a band aid. That also works," his wife said, reaching across the table to pour them each another.

"If we sold the house and moved to a trailer, we could probably buy enough wine for the next ten or fifteen years?" Chris said. But Alice's expression suggested she was about to get serious.

"Look," she said. "For most of your career, you were one of the most respected people in the agency. One of the genuine good guys. That's why I fell in love with you."

"You said that was my 'perfectly sculpted' calf muscles."

"Those too. But seriously—look how unhappy you are. They're letting you rot in some back office. They don't care at all what you've given them. What they've taken from us."

Alice took a long swig of wine, and Chris knew she was trying to stop herself saying something that was unnecessary but inevitable.

"I know it's too late to start a family," she said. "But you still have time to make your life about something other than work."

"Maybe I have time to make it about something other than the CIA," Chris replied. "But now that we're flat broke, I'm still going to need to work."

The room was silent as he noticed the sadness in his

wife's face, knowing it was because she thought they'd never get a chance to spend real time together.

"How about this," Chris said. "I'll quit the agency." His wife's eyes immediately became happier. Happier, maybe, than they had been in years. He'd said many times that he *might* quit, but this was the first time he'd said he would actually do it.

"You're really gonna quit?" she asked.

"Yes, really. Then I'll do a couple years' consulting work, earn more than I could in ten years at the CIA, then we sell the house, buy a little boat, and sail it around the Caribbean. After that, we'll just see where the wind takes us?"

Alice was smiling widely, and Chris thought she might even be about to cry.

"The thing I like most about that," Alice said, "is you get to have a boat again."

"So it's not the fact I'll be out of the agency, or the fact that we won't have to worry about money any more?"

"Well, that does help. But I know how happy sailing makes you. And I'd be pretty happy drinking moonshine in the Caribbean sun."

Alice stood and walked along the table towards Chris. When she reached him, she ran her hand slowly through his hair. She looked into his crystalline blue eyes and paused for a moment to admire them. Then she put her lips to his, and they shared an intense, delicate kiss as feelings they hadn't known for years came flooding back.

CROSSING THE CHAIN BRIDGE

Late autumn sunlight danced on the surface of the Potomac River as Chris crossed the Chain Bridge from the northwest suburbs of D.C. onto George Washington Memorial Parkway. He'd made this journey to CIA Headquarters so many times, but this one was different. This time, he was on his way to inform the Director of his intention to quit the agency. Within a few short weeks, he would be out.

He realized that during the hundreds of times he'd taken this route, through leafy residential areas with large houses and pristine lawns, his thoughts usually followed the same few patterns.

More often than not, he would be thinking obsessively about cases he was working on. Whether he had covered every detail and looked at every one again and again, making sure nothing was left to chance. But no matter how much attention to detail he had paid, there had been times that he couldn't prevent catastrophe. Worries about putting someone at risk during a current case usually led to memories of failing people.

Other times, his mind would turn to a more distant past. Not a past he had experienced, but one he'd learned about. Crossing the Chain Bridge took his mind walking down historical paths.

Most people wouldn't know or care that a bridge was first built in the spot as early as the eighteenth century, and that there had been seven versions since then. In fact, most people would laugh at him for caring how many versions of a certain bridge there had been.

But Chris's unusual lineage, as a distant descendant of the explorer Christopher Columbus, gave him a reason to take an interest in the intricacies of history. He also wondered if his urge to sail came from the same place as his love of history. The difference was that finding the time to sail was much more difficult than idly contemplating history during his drive to work.

If he'd had an argument with his wife, which had been a common occurrence in recent months, his mind would be on that while driving, as he tried to think objectively about who was right or wrong. Then he'd remember that objectivity and marital arguments don't mix.

One thing he never thought about, it now occurred to him, was the future. The complexities of the past and the difficulties of the present, often. But the future, never. He hoped that was about to change.

He cleared security and entered the grounds of the George Bush Center for Intelligence, the CIA

Headquarters complex colloquially known as Langley. He walked past the Original Headquarters Building, subconsciously noting as he always did the oddly Soviet-style starkness of its architecture, then strode past carefully chosen sculptures surrounding the modern New Headquarters Building.

Not that Chris's current role befitted any of HQs imposing presence or proud history. Since his demotion, he'd been consigned to a tiny office far from where any decision-making took place. But today, as he kicked boxes of files around the floor to make enough space to walk to his desk, he didn't care. He ditched his coat and briefcase, then headed immediately to the Director's office.

He was unsure how Helen Miller would react to his news. The two of them went way back. Over a decade ago, they'd been out in the field together as Operations Officers, first in the Middle East then in Central America. She might be sad to see him go from a personal point of view, but it was unlikely she would now miss the services of someone who spent his day kicking boxes around to make enough floor space.

It had been Helen that had demoted him, but she didn't have much choice. He'd gone on an unsanctioned mission to Cuba against her explicit instructions. It was only because a few newspapers got hold of the story and spun it in a good light—the CIA hero who went to Cuba under his own steam to rescue a friend—that he hadn't been fired immediately.

Chris knocked on the polished mahogany door of Helen's office. This was a situation in which most people, even senior figures in the CIA, would have been plucking up courage. Such was Helen's reputation. Even though she was a little shorter than average, her demeanor gave her the appearance of being tall. Chris was taller than average, but fearing Helen less than others did had nothing to do with that. He'd seen her at her most vulnerable, in situations most people couldn't imagine.

The door slowly opened and Helen stood behind it, her thin-lipped expression not changing when she saw Chris.

"Come in," she said coldly.

"I know junior staff members don't generally just pop in here, but I have something important to tell you," Chris said. Helen threw him a look that suggested she didn't enjoy the mild sarcasm, then motioned for him to sit.

"So what do you want to tell me?" she asked, getting straight to the point. At one time, they would have had the rapport to share a bit of banter, maybe even enquire about the health of each other's loved ones. Chris wasn't sure if that had disappeared because she was pissed about Cuba or because she was now taking such a devoted approach to the directorship that she didn't have time for friendliness.

"I'm handing in my resignation," Chris said. "I'll put it in writing soon, of course. But I wanted to tell you in person."

Helen nodded slowly.

"Okay," she said, showing little emotion. "Well, of

course we'll be sad to lose you. But you have to do what's best for you."

"Thank you," Chris said. "I think I've gone as far as I can with the agency. In fact, I'm now going backwards."

Helen paused, gently drumming her fingers on the desk as she looked at Chris. The air was suddenly thick with the tension of two people who have had so many ups and downs they don't know how they're supposed to feel about each other.

"I won't forget what you did for me in Honduras," Helen said. "When we were locked up in that hell hole, you always put on a brave face and reassured me. Even though you must have been suffering too. And you saved your water for me when I was sick. Most people wouldn't do that."

"Well, thank God we somehow both got out of there alive, that's all that matters," Chris replied.

Helen stood up, her hand outstretched. Chris stood too, and they shook hands.

"What will you do?" she asked.

"I'll have to do some serious earning before anything, probably with a private security firm. But after that, I want to do some serious sailing."

"Well, don't let me keep you from earning the big bucks," Helen said as she opened the door. "You can be out of here in less than a month as far as I'm concerned."

Chris saw her thin-lipped expression had returned. Any affection had quickly evaporated like sea spray in the Caribbean breeze.

5

I QUIT

C hris turned onto 16th St NW, taking a brief moment to look to his left to where the White House stood venerably behind the trees of Lafayette Square. Above it, the obelisk of the Washington Monument stood tall, silently symbolizing the remarkable achievements of the nation.

Tallest structure in the world until 1889, Chris thought to himself, then smiled as he thought about how much the man he was about to meet loved to mock him for knowing such trivia.

He entered the stately Hay-Adams hotel and headed through to the Off the Record bar. The bar's genteel decor, with its deep-red tones and plush leather seating, somehow caused its customers to talk in quieter voices no matter how high their status. And given where the bar was located, at the heart of power in the nation's capital, there were plenty of high-status customers.

Chris spotted Ned Henry sitting at a table beside the bar's ornate fireplace.

"Why the hell did we have to come here?" Chris said unceremoniously as he sat.

"I'm great, thanks. How are you?" Ned replied.

"Sorry. How are you?"

"I'm drinking, so I'm fine."

"Well I'm glad to hear it," Chris said, noticing that his friend's alcohol-flushed face was the same color as the red leather seating. "So, why did you have to pick here?" He asked again.

"For a date," Ned replied.

Chris paused. Then said:

"But seriously, what's the real reason?"

"Seriously, that is the real reason." Ned replied. "I had a date with a real-life woman."

"Wow," Chris said, sitting back in his chair. "Congrats. A romantic date in one of D.C.'s most refined bars—I bet you even showered didn't you?"

"I did, but I wasn't happy about it."

Chris took a sip of Glenlivet single malt before he told Ned his big news. Ned was a CIA analyst who had helped Chris from afar on many of his missions. Even back when he had been a Staff Operations Officer, Ned did most of his work from the relative safety of a Langley office while linking up remotely to assist agents out in the field, but that didn't detract from how important his help had been.

"Well …" Chris said. "I quit the agency."

Ned looked at him, searching his face for giveaways.

"You're … you're shitting me?" Ned asked.

"No, hand on heart," Chris said, smiling.

"You finally did it!" Ned said, smiling back.

"Yeah, man."

"Waiter! Champagne!" Ned shouted at a man in black pants and a crisp white shirt.

"The hell you say to me?" the man replied.

"Oh, you don't work here. Sorry, dude," Ned said. The man walked back to his seat while fixing Ned with a stare.

"We'll get champagne in a moment," Ned said. "So, what are you gonna do now?"

"I'll have to do some consulting work for a while," Chris explained. "To say money is tight is an understatement."

"Yeah, 'cause those frat kids took every dime in compensation after you crashed into their boat."

Chris gave Ned a sarcastic smile. His red-faced friend was the only person who knew for sure what happened that day, because he had been on the boat with Chris. The frat boys had smashed into them at high speed, attacked them, then later claimed compensation for their boat, violence that they started, and made-up psychological damage.

"Yes, effectively I'm going to be working the next two years to put some kids I don't know through college."

"And after that?" Ned asked.

"After that, new boat, Caribbean, cocktails at sunset."

"Beautiful, man. Make sure you take some rum. You know how much I love a Planter's Punch."

"I was thinking of taking Alice. Sorry to break it to you."

"Ah. Well, she deserves it," Ned said, grinning. "So do you. Wouldn't be right if your strongest memories of being on the waves were the navy and a bullshit compensation claim."

Their conversation was interrupted by a raised voice from a nearby table.

"God, I *love* that guy!" a young woman exclaimed. She was staring up at a TV where Matthew McGoldrick's chiseled face was on the screen. The candidate was smiling as he clasped hands with well-wishers.

"God, I hate that guy," Ned said. "The glare from his teeth is gonna give me retina damage."

"Yeah," Chris agreed idly, as he browsed the extensive whiskey menu."

"I'll get that champagne," Ned said, taking his phone out of his pocket to check the time. "Whoa! That I did not expect!" he added.

Chris looked up from the menu.

"What?" he asked.

"My date. Marylin. Says she 'literally' can't wait to see me again. Wants to see me right now."

"Excellent!" Chris replied.

"Nah, this is your big night. I'm not just gonna up and leave."

"Go, man," Chris insisted. I've got a lady waiting for me too."

"What? Who?"

"My wife."

"Oh. Yeah. You sure?"

"Yeah, go!"

Ned grinned like a school-kid.

"I can't believe she's this into me!" he said.

"You should have more faith in yourself," Chris told him. "There are plenty of good reasons for women to be into you."

"Yeah, you see it on all the dating sites: must have a good sense of humor and sweat buckets," Ned replied, before standing and throwing a bunch of notes on the table. "Thanks for understanding, man. I'll buy champagne next time for sure."

Ned walked out of the bar, leaving Chris shaking his head and smiling. He finished the last of his Glenlivet and headed out.

As he walked through the lobby of the Hay-Adams, he saw an impeccably dressed couple walking arm in arm towards the bar, laughing loudly and looking like they'd already had a few drinks. He decided that when he got home, he'd open one of the fine Italian reds he had been saving for years and enjoy it with his wife. Just drink, laugh, and look forward rather than back.

As he passed through the stone archway of the hotel's main entrance, he locked eyes with a man walking into the hotel. A cold shiver of recognition ran down his spine. He'd only seen the man briefly, but he was trained not to forget faces. He was 99 percent certain it was Basem Lellouche. That had been the agency's best guess at his real name, at least. He went by many.

Lellouche was a hitman Chris had encountered in

North Africa more than a decade ago. But he wasn't only a hitman—he was notorious for taking people out in the most shocking ways imaginable to instill fear in the enemies of whoever acquired his services. He specialized in butchering his clients' political opponents.

The guy shouldn't even have been able to enter the United States. Not legally. But Chris was sure it was him. The crooked nose and the lifeless eyes. Very few people had eyes like that.

He desperately wanted to walk away and forget what he'd seen, but he knew that wasn't possible. With his heart sinking, he turned and walked back into the hotel.

6

ONE OF THE GOOD GUYS

In the lobby of the Hay-Adams, with Bach playing softly in the background, Chris waited for Basem Lellouche. Facing away from the center of the lobby, he used the reflection in the highly polished metal of an enormous vase to watch people come and go.

It had been more than an hour since he'd seen Basem walking into the hotel, and the elapsing minutes had given the alcohol Chris had been enjoying earlier time to wear off. Finally, the unmistakably stocky figure of Basem appeared in the reflection. Chris watched him leave the hotel, then waited twenty seconds before following.

The conditions for trailing someone were good. It was dark, but the streets were still busy enough to leave people between himself and Basem. It wasn't ideal that the guy had met his gaze when they'd passed at the hotel, but if he'd done things correctly back in North Africa, Basem should never have seen his face. Chris, however, was well aware that Basem might know who he was simply because he'd been a senior figure in the CIA.

Basem turned onto Connecticut Avenue, and Chris followed sixty meters behind, the chilly fall air providing a good reason to tuck his head into his collar. Past buzzing bars and restaurants with chattering customers behind misty windows, Basem walked unwaveringly, never pausing to look around. He took a right and then, still looking nowhere but dead straight ahead, strode into The Jefferson hotel.

He walked across the checkered marble floor of the hotel lobby to where receptionists were waiting with a smile to help. Chris pushed the button for an elevator and kept his face turned away from reception as he tried to hear what Basem was saying. The only phrase he picked up, or thought he had, was "…his driver is here."

Seconds later, he heard heavy footsteps coming towards the elevators. He pushed the button hard again as he watched the gold arrow tick lethargically down the floor numbers. There were three elevators, and he wanted to end up in a different one from Basem. He pushed the up button once more, gambling that Basem would be going down towards the parking lot. Finally, the elevator arrived. The doors opened painfully slowly, revealing two elderly couples who dawdled as they made their way out while joking about the cost of the minibar.

Chris entered and heard a shuffle as somebody followed him in. His heart was beating hard as he turned to face the front. The only other person in the elevator was a young woman in an evening gown, and for once

Chris was glad to see such a garish outfit. He went up a few floors then immediately pushed to go down to the basement.

The darkness of the basement would provide some cover, but Chris was now highly alert and extremely cautious. He exited the elevator and moved close to the far wall, pushing himself against the cold surface as he made his way to the end of the corridor that led into the parking lot. He moved his head just far enough to see around the corner, and his eyes landed on Basem standing beside a silver Lincoln Continental a few parking spaces away. He was talking with another man who had his back to Chris. He could just about hear their angry whispers.

"What the hell do you need to see me for?" the other man hissed at Basem.

"I wanted to give you the proof in person," Basem replied, slipping something tiny into the man's coat pocket.

"What do I need proof for? Just do your job."

"Because last time, you didn't pay me. This time, you have no excuse."

"Don't ever come near me again," the man growled at Basem. "Get out of the country and don't contact me."

"Chill the fuck out," Basem said, smiling as he opened the car door. "Nobody here knows who I am."

The man said nothing as he turned to walk away, revealing his face to Chris. It was Matthew McGoldrick.

Chris immediately turned away. He saw a stairwell next to the elevator and skipped up it quickly, leaving the elevators free for McGoldrick. He made his way up the dark stairwell until he saw a sign saying 'Lobby.' He smartened himself up and walked back into the lobby with the calm air of a man on his way to dinner.

"I'm here for Senator McGoldrick's reception," he said to the woman on the front desk. "Could you tell me which room?"

"It's in the Great Room, sir," she said, pointing across the lobby. Down this corridor on the left and right to the end. You can't miss it."

Chris thanked her and walked towards the Great Room, formulating a plan as he went. He could see the evening was winding down. Waiters were carrying out trays of empty glasses. But there were still a couple security guys on the door.

"Chris Collins," he said when he got to the entrance, looking down at a guest list that did not contain his name. "Hope I'm not too late for the free stuff!"

"Your name's not on the list," the nearest security guard said gruffly.

"I didn't give you my name because it's on the list, I gave you it because you should know who I am," he replied, flashing his CIA ID.

"He's the Deputy Director," the other doorman said.

"Sorry, sir," the first told Chris, who was happy for them to believe he still held that position.

He glanced across the ballroom to where McGoldrick was smiling widely as he chatted with an attractive woman, calling over a waiter to top up her champagne.

"Don't worry," Chris heard him saying as he approached, "I decide when this wraps up, not them."

Chris's elbow nudged into the woman's arm hard enough to make her drink spill on McGoldrick, who let out a brief angry shout before turning the charm back on and telling the woman not to worry.

"I'm so sorry, that was my fault," Chris said as he brushed champagne from McGoldrick's jacket.

"Chris Collins," McGoldrick said. Chris gave him an affirmative nod. "One of Washington's few good guys, I hear," the Senator added.

"Well, it's a low bar sometimes," Chris replied, smiling.

"Should I get some more champagne?" the woman asked.

"No, this is wrapping up," McGoldrick replied. "Pleasure to meet you, if briefly," he said to Chris as he shook his hand. "Sorry I didn't meet you earlier in the evening, there were a lot of people to meet and greet."

"Not a problem," Chris said. "And again, apologies for the drink."

They went their separate ways and Chris headed out of the hotel, a newly acquired USB stick in his pocket.

He noticed the temperature had dropped a couple of degrees as he walked out into the night. There could be no acceptable explanation for McGoldrick meeting Basem, he thought as he headed to the subway station to take him home. He wanted to get a look at what was on that USB as soon as possible.

7

SHATTERED WINDOW

In his dimly lit study, Chris took a sip of whiskey and steeled himself for what he might see on the USB stick. Normally, if he had some late-night work to do, he would take his laptop and sit with his wife in the living room as she finished up some wine. It was the least he could do having been working out in foreign fields for much of his career, before returning to a desk job in D.C. that still took up most of his time. But he didn't want to be around anyone when he opened whatever was on that memory stick.

He knew there was a good chance the contents would be password protected, which would mean he would have to wait a day or two while Ned, his cyber-analyst colleague, worked his magic. But he was also aware that Basem was arrogant, proud of his work, and had total contempt for authority.

Chris clicked open the only file on the stick and found

he had been right about Basem. There were eight immediately viewable images that confirmed Basem was not only as arrogant as Chris suspected, but as brutal as well.

A young man, only nineteen or twenty years old, was in all of the pictures. It looked like he had died after being beaten and tortured. There were slashes across his face and upper torso, and he had been blinded in both eyes.

Chris sat back in his chair, processing what he was looking at. He took a long sip of whiskey and drew it slowly into his body. Then he took his phone from his pocket and dialed.

"Chris," Helen said, sounding tired and a little concerned. "What's wrong?"

"I need to show you something," Chris replied. "I know it's late, but we need to get on this. I'm emailing you now."

"Give me a minute," Helen said.

"You see it?" Chris asked after a pause. Helen waited a long time before responding.

"Yeah."

"That's from a memory stick I took from Senator McGoldrick. Without his knowledge, of course. It was handed to him by a man named Basem Lellouche, a hitman I first encountered years ago in North Africa."

"McGoldrick?" Helen asked.

"Yes, Matthew McGoldrick. He's involved in something. We need to find out what, but first I need you to put all nearby ports on alert for Lellouche leaving the country."

Helen paused again, and Chris hoped it was because she was tired and a little stunned—possibly drunk—and not because she resented being given orders.

"Helen?"

"I'm on it," she replied. "We'll get on the McGoldrick connection first thing tomorrow. Right now, I'll make sure Basem doesn't leave the country."

Chris hung up, then fired off a message to his friend, Ned Henry, letting him know what he'd found out about McGoldrick and Basem. He knew Ned would start looking into both men right away, and he felt grateful that he could always rely on him with no ego or bullshit involved.

THE NEXT MORNING, Chris was driving across the Chain Bridge once again. It was a gorgeously sunny morning, one on which he should have been feeling happy about his future prospects and leaving the past behind. But all of that now seemed far away.

He turned onto George Washington Memorial Parkway in an area flanked by woodland. As his thoughts turned for the hundredth time to why McGoldrick might be involved with Basem, a violent noise exploded into his ears, the back end of his car spinning to the left as he gripped the wheel tight. He wrestled with the car but he couldn't keep control. A tree was suddenly right in front of him and he slammed hard into it, putting his arm up at the last minute to protect his face from shattering glass.

While he was still in a daze, the driver side window shattered too, seconds before a fist crashed into his jaw. He flung the door open, forcing the attacker backwards and giving himself time to get out. But his head was spinning, and as soon as he stepped from the car the attacker was back on him, dragging him into the trees.

Another crushing blow landed on the side of Chris's head and he hit the ground. The smell of soil filled his nostrils and he felt a heavy body on top of his, a knee pushing hard into his back. He tried to push himself up, but this was a big guy and he couldn't shake him. Then the weight was abruptly lifted and the body moved away. Chris staggered to his feet to see a bulky man running back towards the cars.

Chris was on him just as he reached his vehicle, and the man turned back to face him. Chris swung his right arm and felt bones crunch as he landed an elbow on the man's chin. The guy growled but stayed on his feet, and his face was now an inch from Chris's. The two of them were locked in a tussle, and Chris gritted his teeth as he mustered the strength to release himself from the man's grip. Then, he realized his left arm was locked with the big man's, and he twisted it and pushed up with all his strength. The man shrieked as his arm broke.

Chris was rusty and had rarely been in situations like this for years. Past training was kicking in and he was getting on top, but whoever this guy was, he was young, strong, and an experienced fighter. Chris threw two palm strikes to the guy's face and felt his nose break, but the man had hold of Chris's collar and wasn't letting go.

Chris knew what was coming and tried to dodge it, but a brutal headbutt landed right on his forehead. The world went black and he fell backwards, out cold before he hit the ground.

8

BATTERY

Chris was brought gently back to consciousness by the rhythmic beeping of hospital machinery. He slowly opened his eyes and saw a nurse bringing in a tray of food.

"Ah!" she said cheerfully. "You're alive!"

"I'm afraid so," he replied. "Sorry that makes your day busier."

The nurse smiled and put the tray in front of him.

"I'm not sure I can face that," he said. "What's the damage?"

"Broken nose, broken collarbone, severe concussion," she told him.

He thought back to what had happened. He didn't remember the guy targeting his collarbone, so that must have happened in the initial crash. The fact that he'd given the guy a good fight even with a broken collarbone made him feel a little better. But he knew his skills weren't what they used to be. And he knew the memory stick was gone.

He tried to remember the man's face, but there was nothing very distinctive. Thick eyebrows, bad teeth.

"Can I use my phone?" he asked the nurse. She brought him his phone from a locker in the corner then judiciously left the room.

He called Helen.

"Chris," she said.

"No, I'm fine, please don't worry yourself," he replied curtly. "Any news on Basem?"

"He hasn't been spotted going through any ports."

"The guy who attacked me this morning?"

"Car found at the scene so he must have escaped on foot. Rental vehicle probably hired with fake ID."

"Shit," Chris said. "He took the memory stick. What's the next move? I assume you're dealing with this?"

"The only international element to this is Basem," Helen said. "This is FBI business."

"Okay, so what are they doing?"

"Not a lot right now. There were only two things they could act on, the memory stick and your witness statement. But if you give a statement, it isn't going to hold much credibility now."

"What do you mean?"

"You haven't seen the news?"

"No, I've been out cold. It's hard to keep track of current events when you're unconscious. Would you please tell me what's going on?"

"I'm sorry," Helen said, "but it's not my place to talk

you through it all. Alice is on her way to see you right now, she knows what's happening."

"Helen, what the hell is going on?" Chris replied, bewildered.

"Just talk to Alice. And save me the trouble of suspending you by using your personal leave and retiring early. We'll sort out the details later."

Chris was no longer feeling the pain of his injuries.

I need to know what's happening before I talk to Alice, he thought. *I'm not going to make her tell me everything.*

Reluctantly, he opened the browser on his phone and went to CNN.

Ex-CIA Deputy Director Accused of Battery.

Chris scanned the headline rapidly before reading on, his heart hammering in his chest.

Chris Collins, the former Deputy Director of the CIA, is wanted for police questioning after allegedly beating a woman 'half to death' during what appears to have been an encounter with an escort.

Collins, who is due to retire from the agency shortly, is suspected of aggravated battery against the unnamed victim, who said she was with him at an apartment close to the Hay-Adams hotel in Downtown D.C. on Tuesday night.

Last night? Chris thought to himself. *When I spent periods alone without an alibi and also saw McGoldrick in a compromising situation?* It dawned on him immediately what was going on. He pushed redial hard.

"Chris, I've told you what your status is professionally, and you'll compromise me personally if you keep calling me," Helen told him.

"You can't believe this shit, surely? It's obviously a set-up."

"McGoldrick has an absolutely immaculate record."

"So do I."

"Until recently, you did. Then you got into an embarrassing compensation battle after getting into a fight with college kids, and you went on a rogue mission to Cuba where you tarnished not only your own reputation but the agency's too."

"Screw you. It's being tarnished by people like you putting political sensitivity before victims."

"Yeah? Well, screw you too. And just so you know, the consensus at the FBI is that you've lost your shit, so don't expect any help from them. Get a lawyer."

Helen hung up.

Chris threw his head back in disbelief as he dialed his wife. Before she had answered, he made up his mind. He wasn't going to wait for the police, who were likely on their way to the hospital. He wasn't going to wait months to be tried for a crime that he had been framed for by a powerful politician whose word everyone would believe.

"Alice," he said when his wife answered.

"Chris, what the hell is going on? Who is that woman?"

"Don't cry," Chris told her, hearing that her voice was trembling. "You've got to keep your wits about you. This is a setup. You know none of it's true, right?"

"I know," she replied, quietly.

"Good. You've got to leave town. Get out of state, you know where to go. Where you'll be safe."

"Where are you going?"

"I can't tell you right now."

"You're leaving me?"

"I'll be leaving for much longer if I don't figure this all out, just trust me. Please."

As he said goodbye to his wife and finished the call, Chris was already unhooking himself from the medical gear around him. He grimaced as he stood, then went to the locker and took what few belongings he had.

Exiting the room, he turned away from where two nurses were talking down the corridor to his left, and headed to the quieter far end. He ignored the elevators and aimed for the fire exit, growling in pain as he pushed the bar down and shoulder charged the stiff door open.

He limped as quickly as he could down the chilly staircase and emerged onto the street. He took a look around and realized he was in Annandale, several miles southwest of CIA HQ.

He ducked into an underpass that stank of piss and seemed to be used mostly by homeless people. He walked beside a murky stream along a gravel path that would be helpful in alerting him to any footsteps behind. For now, it was quiet.

He took out his phone and called Ned, who offered no greeting.

"Don't ever call me again. I always knew you were sick in the head," he said abruptly.

"I'm going to assume you're joking."

"You assume right. Sorry."

"All good, joking around helped us through darker situations than this."

"This is pretty dark though, man. The media are going to town—you're their cash cow 'til the next story comes along."

"I know. Not going to be easy to lie low around here. That's why I need your help."

"I thought you might say that. I assumed it wasn't your plan to wait around to get arrested."

"So what you got?"

"Our friend, tonight."

"Our friend The Drinker or our friend The Fighter?"

"The Drinker. The Fighter is not who you need right now. You know where to go—exact details to follow."

"Thanks, Ned. I can't tell you how much I appreciate this."

"You got it. Our friend will tell you what to do on the other side. I might be offline for a while—getting fired I could live with, but prison I cannot take."

"Understood, buddy. And thanks again."

Emerging onto a busy road, Chris flagged down a cab. He told the driver to head for downtown Baltimore. It was a four-hour walk from where he needed to be, but giving away his exact destination was too risky.

Ten minutes into the journey, Chris could see the driver eyeing him through the rearview mirror.

"You that guy from the news?" the driver asked, his curiosity getting the better of his professionalism.

"Which guy?"

"Guy with the escort woman."

"You're asking if I beat up women?"

The driver looked embarrassed.

"No, sir."

"Maybe I look like him, I don't know. But what I do know is, the best way to drive is with your eyes on the road."

"Yes, sir."

Chris exited the cab in downtown Baltimore and looked at his phone. A message from Ned simply read:

Clearwater Pier. Midnight.

He deleted the message and began walking southeast, making his way towards North Point State Park on the shore of Chesapeake Bay. Night was already falling by the time he reached the suburbs of East Baltimore. Some of the suburbs were run down and were home to a few people who fixed him with who-the-hell-are-you stares, which he returned unflinchingly, forcing them to look away. It was a skill he had never forgotten.

By the time he reached the leafy, affluent neighborhoods near the coast, where people still had a who-the-hell-are-you attitude but lacked the balls to stare, it was almost midnight.

The lights of residential communities disappeared as he approached the park. He could see the twinkling lights of ships out in Chesapeake Bay, and hoped some of them belonged to the vessel he was bound for.

He trudged past wetlands and pockets of tall trees reaching up towards the moon and stars that provided his only source of light. Some of the trees swallowed up the ruined buildings that once belonged to Bay Shore Park, an abandoned amusement park that was once much loved but was now decaying.

Finally, he reached the coastline, and next to a tiny pier of crumbling concrete, he stepped into the cover of the trees … and waited.

NO ENGLISH

In a tiny, humid apartment in Yangon, Myanmar, Tsu stood over the man she had heaved back like a drunk companion, mouthing the Burmese word for 'drunk' to an occasional passerby. Now, he had a rope around his chest and was tied to a chair in her kitchen.

She fixed him with a look that made clear she was not here to screw around. The man stared back at her beautiful face—with its flawless pale skin and high cheekbones framed by silken black hair—bewildered by the contradiction in front of him.

"Why did you kill him?" Tsu asked.

"No English."

"Give me a name. They're the same in any language."

"Fuck you."

"That's English, you're doing better. Who sent you?"

"Que kaung!"

Tsu knew Burmese well enough to know the man was

still insulting her. She shoved his face into the red heat of the cooking hob, leaving it there as layer after layer of skin sizzled away. The man screamed. Tsu kept his face on the ring for a few extra seconds, then yanked it up. She walked across her rented apartment and turned up the TV.

She returned to the kitchen, rummaged around in a cupboard, and pulled out a bottle of bleach. She twisted off the cap and waved the bottle at the man.

"Please," he said, his bottom lip trembling slightly. "They just send photo and address. Really."

By now, Tsu had met enough scumbags to know when they were lying or not. She decided that part was true.

"Who's 'they'?"

"I don't know. Many people. It's just a job."

Tsu picked up the phone she'd taken from the man's pocket.

"Pin code."

"No."

She moved his face towards the heat again, then held the bottle over his head to within one degree of pouring."

"Okay!" the man shouted. 5-9-3-0!"

She tapped in the code, and a screensaver of the man with three smiling young kids appeared.

"Family?" she asked. The man nodded. Tsu looked at him and saw how gaunt he was. This wasn't a big-time gangster with a lavish lifestyle.

"I'm going to let you go," she said. But if you tell anyone I'm looking for them, I'll find you and cut out your tongue."

The man didn't respond, so she took a large kitchen knife from a drawer, then prized open his mouth and pulled out his tongue from between brown and yellow teeth.

"Tongue," she said slowly, holding the blade so it was just touching his flesh. "Cut. Just in case you forgot your English again."

The man nodded, wide-eyed and terrified. Tsu cut the tie on his legs, then without saying another word she marched him through her apartment, opened the door, and threw him out so hard he slammed into the far wall of the corridor.

IN THE TWO months she had been living there, Tsu had noticed that Yangon, Myanmar's capital, always had a strange quietness about it. As if the people were permanently cautious. *It's a city full of contrasts*, she thought, as she made her way across town. People on the street were quiet and nervous while around them the roar of outdated engines from cars and scooters filled the air. The colorful British colonial buildings had their brightness dampened by gray dust, and the gold domes and spires of magnificent temples towered over a city where most people live close to poverty.

Right now, she was thinking about the contrast of the obviously poor man who had killed Marco being paid to do the dirty work of much richer men. It was those richer men that she—and Marco before he was killed—had been assigned to track down in Yangon. So far, they had drawn blanks, which wasn't surprising considering how little they had to go on. An arms dealer known only as Nabyr, probably a pseudonym, had popped up in the city, according to one of their assets. But they had been given no physical description or nationality, and he had proved a difficult man to find.

But the phone taken from the man in her apartment had provided a clue. The most recent message, sent along with a picture of Marco, had been in Assamese script. She realized the man she'd dragged to her apartment had the look of somebody from northeastern India, possibly the state of Assam. Whoever was giving him instructions was likely also Assamese.

As the sun was setting, its light filtering to soft reds through the layer of pollution over the city, Tsu was making her way towards the Little India district. It was a place to start.

During brief restful moments, she had noticed yet another contrast, of people sitting on plastic stools outside simple roadside eateries that served food more complex and delicious than some of the world's best restaurants. These places were bustling and full right now, but she had no time to think about dinner. She was about to turn on the charm.

The fact that so many men seemed to find her attractive was something Tsu had struggled with, but often used to her advantage. An important part of her job was getting information from people. Hurting people was effective, but it was also bad for the soul. Charming people wasn't easygoing on the soul either, but at least it varied things up a little.

She walked past a garishly colorful temple onto a narrow street with shops and food stalls looking like they were almost piled on top of each other. She was looking for a bar called The Foxhole—the only bar in Little India. She knew that bars are places where people talk more easily.

She spotted the name on a faded sign hanging over a narrow entrance. She ducked inside and entered a small, dark room with cluttered decor featuring everything from 1950s Guinness posters to statues of Hindu deities. It was still early evening, and the place was empty except for the bartender. She took a seat at the end of the bar and ordered a Scotch.

The bartender, a man in his late twenties with a thin but strong frame, was trying to catch glimpses of her as he made the drink, resisting the urge to stare.

"It's quiet tonight," she said when he brought over the Scotch.

"Yes. There will probably be more people later."

She looked down at her drink, slowly twisting the heavy glass on the counter.

"I'll need you to keep me entertained then," she told the bartender. "I hope you're okay with that?"

"Yes!" he said. "No problem. Where are you from?"

"Guess," Tsu replied, curling her lips into a teasing smile. It didn't matter if he guessed right or not … she wouldn't confirm it. She didn't give unnecessary details to close associates, let alone strangers. But it was a way to get him talking.

"Japan?" he asked.

"No, but close."

"South Korea?"

"Close again, but wrong."

He paused, taking the time to gaze at her face.

"North Korea?"

"That was a waste of a guess," Tsu said. "And now you're out."

"Already?"

"I'm afraid so. Now, it's my turn. I'm going to guess you're not from Myanmar … "

It didn't take much more talking—a short discussion about when the man had emigrated from India and a brief compliment about how he looked too athletic to be working in a bar—before he was at her mercy. Encouraging him to have a few drinks from his own bar also helped.

"Hey, I need some excitement," Tsu said as they clinked another round.

"What kind of excitement?"

"You're a barman. Barmen hear things, right?"

"Sometimes."

"Who are the big players around here? The gangsters, criminals."

"Why do you want to know that?" the bartender asked, his face growing serious.

"I guess I watch too many movies, but it interests me."

The man shrugged.

"Mostly it's just small-time," he said. "I heard there was some new guy on the scene, making big moves. I don't know his name though."

"That's usually when things get interesting in the movies," Tsu said. "Turf wars."

"I guess so."

"So, tell me more!"

"Someone told me he's running a jazz club down by the river. But that's probably not the real reason he's here. I don't know."

"Okay, obviously you're not going to give me any gruesome details," Tsu replied, throwing him a look of mock disappointment. "Hey, do you want to get dinner some time?"

"Sure!" the man said, looking delighted.

"Great!" I can't do it tonight, but I'll come back soon."

"I'll look forward to it," the bartender said, softening his eyes to give her his best seductive look. But it landed on the back of her head, and she was gone.

10

PRIMARY ORDER

Cigar smoke drifted up among the droplets of a crystal chandelier. A man with pitted skin and bloated jowls was looking up and watching the smoke as it dispersed, allowing himself to be distracted from the conversation he was having.

"Never start smoking, kid," the man told a younger person sitting across an ornate mahogany desk from him. "I wouldn't want to set a bad example to you."

The young man laughed. The cigar smoker smiled, and added:

"I'll teach you how to jack people up. I have no problem with that. I just don't want you smoking."

"Speaking of jacking people up," the young man said, sweeping his French-cropped blond hair to one side. "Collins is on the run."

"I know. You say that like it's something to be happy about."

"Isn't it?"

"No, it's not. We had him right where we wanted him: broke, embarrassed, and about to retire. He would have been a non-entity. The only thing better would have been if he was dead. But now, he is a problem again. He may be on the run, but he is angry. It's also more difficult for us to keep an eye on him."

"I don't know what's so important about the guy anyways," the kid said, spilling a little red wine on his Yale tank top as he gestured.

"Hey! That's a thousand a bottle. You ever do that kind of embarrassing shit at a Skull and Bones meeting and I'll make sure they throw you out. Even though I got you in."

The kid shrugged.

"What's so important," the man continued, "is that Collins is both talented and incorruptible. That's exactly the kind of person we don't need standing in our way. And now, he won't stop until he finds out what's going on. McGoldrick, that imbecile, has really screwed us."

"He panicked," the kid said.

"Damn right he did. Now pass me another cigar. And take one for yourself."

"I thought you told me not to smoke?"

"I did. But I also told you not to take orders from anyone. Not anyone, ever."

"Even you?"

"Even me," the jowled man said. "But if you ever disobey me, I'll kill you." He let out a laugh that rumbled among the smokey mucus at the back of his throat.

"I don't know what the hell you're even talking about now," his son said. "I'm guessing it's some kind of test."

"You're damn right it's a test. Pass me that cigar. Light it up for me, but do not inhale. Then, get McGoldrick on the phone."

The kid picked up a phone from the desk and dialed. When McGoldrick answered, the kid ignored him and passed the phone to his father.

"Fucking idiot," the jowled man said.

"What have I done now?" McGoldrick asked.

"Letting Collins see you in a compromising situation, that's what."

"I already apologized to you for that."

"I know, but I am simply reminding you that you're a fucking idiot. And an apology is not good enough. Nowhere near. This is going to cause me all kinds of grief. Someone, somewhere will have to take him out, but we don't even know where he's headed to."

"We'll get him."

"You're so sure, why? Just get the word out to anyone you know that he needs to be taken out."

"That will compromise me even more."

"Your campaign? You're whining about your campaign? Don't forget you wouldn't be where you are if it wasn't for me."

"Like you're doing me a favor," McGoldrick hissed.

"Talk to me like that again and your sordid story will be on the front page of the *New York Times* by morning. You piece of shit."

Stressed by the insults and his situation, McGoldrick lost his temper.

"Why don't you just let me get on with my life?" he growled. "I'll help you when I'm in power, but I'm not your bitch. You don't control me."

"That's exactly what you are, and that's exactly what I do," the man said. "I know what you did in Brooklyn, and I have the evidence. Don't ever forget it." He hung up the phone.

"My primary order to you is to never end up like that guy," he told his son.

"What did he do in Brooklyn?"

"He told the press he found a woman drugged and beaten on the street, and helped her. They called him a hero, and it gave him a giant boost in his political career. Except it was him that drugged her and him that beat her, and she never even knew about it. Only I knew about it, because like a lot of other D.C. suits, I had him bugged."

"Biggest mistake he ever made," the son said.

"It was many years ago," his father replied. "But it will live with him forever. Ruined him, but did me a big favor. That's how this shit works."

11

ZODIAC RIDE

Cold was beginning to seep into Chris's bones as he waited patiently and silently on the rugged coastline of North Point State Park. Midnight was the time he should have been picked up, but that had long gone. He was scanning the water for activity and listening for the sound of an engine.

The problem was, anything he saw or heard could be either friendly or hostile—the people Ned had sent to get him, or law enforcement already on his tail. He was scanning the dark water of Chesapeake Bay yet again when he heard a distant buzz. He figured the size of the engine meant it was a small speedboat, possibly as small as a Navy Combat Rubber Raiding Craft—a Zodiac as most people knew it. Even if the people on board were friendly, a boat like that wouldn't get him very far. But in this situation, he had to take what he was given.

The sound of the engine grew louder, and was joined by the lapping of waves as he caught sight of the boat.

There was no doubt it was heading in his direction. He couldn't make out the faces of the two men on board, and by the time he could, it would be too late to run. He just had to hope.

The boat slowed as it approached the shore, and Chris stared hard. He didn't recognize either of the people, and his instinct was telling him to run even though that would only make his situation worse. In the end, oddly, it was a cough that he recognized. A rhythmic cough followed by an aggressive throat clearance, like the guy was trying to clear forty years of booze and tobacco out of his body.

The man held out his hand, and finally Chris's eyes confirmed that it was Jackie McShane. The two of them had met many years ago, when they first joined the navy. Chris grasped the hand and shook it firmly without saying a word, both men smiling in the dark. He stepped into the boat, and it immediately turned around and sped out across the water.

As they zipped across the bay, Chris felt momentary exhilaration as he was taken suddenly back to his navy days. He fought off thoughts of how things were much simpler back then, and how messed up they were now. Instead, he just breathed in the sea air.

Before long, a huge vessel loomed out of the darkness, and Chris could see the gangway being lowered to meet them while the ship was still moving. Their tiny dinghy pulled up alongside the giant cargo ship and Chris stepped out, grabbing the cold metal of the gangway rail.

His sea legs returned before he'd made it up the swaying walkway.

He tossed his burner phone over the side of the ship, watching it slowly fall into the dark water, then stepped onto tattered carpet as he moved inside the vessel. He followed Jackie into a small, very warm saloon with three large bottles of whiskey set on a scratched table. Five glistening, perfectly lined-up tumblers contrasted with the modest surroundings.

"First things first," Jackie announced, twisting the top off a bottle and glugging out two large measures of the brown liquor. "Welcome aboard," he said, clinking glasses with Chris as they sat down on benches of torn leather.

"I didn't recognize you back there," Chris said, noticing his old friend's blond hair looked the same as it did when he was twenty-five, but now hung over a face with canyon-like wrinkles. He looked different from when Chris last saw him, but that was more than ten years earlier.

"Must be your eyes going," Jackie said, raising a finger from his glass to point in Chris's direction.

"Must be," Chris replied. "Desk jobs are more dangerous than the military."

"I knew you'd need my help sooner or later," Jackie said.

"You mean you knew one day I'd end up on the run, my whole life gone to shit?"

"I mean you always had it all—the good looks, the talent. Naval Academy, top of the CIA. Your luck had to run out someday. Everyone's does."

"Well today's the day," Chris said. "Actually, it was yesterday. You were late."

"Worst still," Jackie said, "now you gotta keep pace with me until all this whiskey's gone."

They were already four glasses in when three more guys ducked through the doorway to join them.

"Ah! Our competition winners," Jackie said as the men took their seats. "These three squids are always arguing about who's the best drinker onboard, so now's their chance to find out."

Chris was introduced to the men—all crew members of different nationalities.

"Chien … " Jackie said loudly, jabbing his finger in the direction of one of the men. " … Vietnam! Rayan … France! Lucas … the hell you from again?"

"Sweden."

"I know. Just playin' with you. And this here's Chris Collins. I saved his life a time or two."

"Yeah, it was that way around," Chris said, raising his eyebrows.

"Must've been. You know what they call me, right?"

"You mean to your face?" Chris replied. Everyone laughed except Jackie.

"*The Unkillable*," Jackie informed the room. "The man who cannot be killed."

"The man who cannot be quiet," Lucas stated.

"You know," Chien joined in. "I agree with that old saying: *if you have to tell people you're tough, you're probably not.*"

Jackie pushed his lips upwards and nodded with mock

agreement. He filled up everyone's glasses to the top, then downed his own.

Three glasses later, in the middle of the sea and the middle of the night, rain was hammering against the window. Conversation had turned to the times the various people in the room had come closest to dying. For Chris, it was a firefight in Caracas. For Lucas, a climbing accident in New Zealand that he claimed would have killed most people.

Jackie, though, had seemingly decided those incidents weren't close enough. He rummaged around in a cupboard at the back of the room, pulling out an unmarked bottle of clear liquid.

"Vodka. Ukrainian. It's not legal, but it is the best," he informed the room.

"What do you mean by *the best*?" Chien asked.

"I mean the strongest. 95 percent."

This was not the time for anyone to back out. Jackie poured out the moonshine into the empty whiskey glasses, a tiny amount of the brown whiskey mixing into the clear vodka.

Chris threw his back like everybody else, and felt the spirit immediately begin eating away at the inside of his throat, burning up into his eyes. It was awful. But before he knew it, another glass was ready and waiting. There were five more each before the bottle was finally empty. Attempts at conversation were now futile, and what attempts there were consisted of nonsense rambling.

The clock read 06:10 when Chris pulled himself back from wandering thoughts and looked around the hazy room. Chien and Lucas were asleep on each other, and Rayan, who had said almost nothing all night, had quietly slipped away. Chris looked over at Jackie, who was pointing at him while holding half a glass of whiskey.

"You lose," Jackie slurred, yanking the glass towards his mouth. But he fell asleep mid-swig, dropping the glass. It fell straight onto the table, bottom first, bounced, and miraculously held all of the liquid. It was the last booze in the room, and Chris knew it would be a shame if they'd come that far and left a drop. He looked at the glass for a moment, then reached out, picked it up, and finished it in one go.

He walked out of the booze and tobacco cloud the room had become, and stepped onto the ship's vast deck as the sun was beginning to creep over the horizon. The rain had stopped and the air was calm. Nobody else was around, and only the sound of a few gulls managed to punctuate the droning of the ship's engine.

He thought about how much had changed in just a few short days. People would now think of him as a villain, capable of the kind of messed up shit he'd spent his life fighting. Even though the accusations were false, it was still extremely hard to take.

He stared out at the waves towards the distant coastline, gripping the metal railings tight and trying to come to terms with how many people would now hate him for something he hadn't done. "Screw 'em," he said. But he wasn't sure if he meant it.

12

NEXT: FRANCE

I t had been five days at sea when Chris woke up to another morning with the sun streaming through his cabin window, assaulting his eyes as he realized he would have to deal with yet another hangover.

He had got used to telling Jackie to rein it in after a few drinks, but a few drinks of the stuff Jackie liked was still enough to make anybody feel like death. As they slowly sailed closer to the west coast of Ireland, he knew he would have to put the brakes on the drinking completely. He needed his wits about him.

He picked up the book by the side of his bed, *The Enigma Strain*, judiciously avoiding switching on the satellite TV. He read three pages when there was a heavy knock on his door.

"J wants to see you," said a voice he didn't recognize.

"Got it," he replied. He rolled out of bed and got dressed, sweeping his hair to one side and looking at his reddened eyes in the mirror. Then he made his way through a few of the ship's many passageways to where Jackie was waiting in the saloon.

"How are we feeling?" Jackie asked.

"Like I fought twelve rounds with a heavyweight champion whose wife just left him."

"Well, you need to get your head together, 'cause I got news."

"Yeah?"

"Yeah—message from Ned. First thing: Ireland. When we dock, you're heading for Caldare, a small village. There's a church there where a guy will meet you at 10pm the day we land. He'll ask you something only you should know the answer to.

"Got it."

"Next: France."

"France?"

"You need to get to France as soon as you can—we got a lead there. Basem Lellouche, spotted in Bordeaux a few months back. Was doing some of his usual dirty work but got interrupted and fled, so the victim is still alive."

"It's a start," Chris said.

"Right. It's not much, but it's all you've got. Victim is called Marianne Gigot, she's an actress. Least she was 'til Basem got hold of her."

"So how do I find her?"

"That's still to follow. I called Ned back."

"Called him back?"

"Yeah. I forgot the exact details of how to find her."

"You forgot? What the hell does that mean?"

Jackie never did like being criticized. But before, he never messed up as bad as this.

"I'll take care of it," he said, looking at Chris like he didn't need the hassle.

"Where did you call him back? If it was as easy as just calling him, I could do it myself."

"Called him at work," Jackie said.

"What the hell?" Chris replied. "If they find out he's helping me, he's finished."

"I know, I wasn't thinking."

"You mean you were drunk?"

Jackie fixed Chris with a hard stare.

"Ah, so what," he snarled. "The fat prick would survive without his desk job. Got no family to take care of. If he gets fired, it'll give him more time to eat."

"He could get worse than fired," Chris said, raising his arm and pointing at Jackie. "You're losing your shit."

Jackie whipped his arm through the air and knocked Chris's forearm aside, then swung a punch with his other hand. Chris reacted immediately and ducked before the fist connected with his head. He was about to follow up with a move to subdue Jackie, but the missed punch was enough to knock his old friend off balance. Jackie stumbled into a wall, then grabbed out at Chris's hand to stop himself from falling. With Chris's help, he just about stayed on his feet. Their gaze met very briefly before Jackie walked out of the room, and Chris saw shame and sadness in his eyes.

∾

It was a quiet few days out in the middle of the Atlantic. The drinking sessions had ended, though Jackie probably still had his own in private. Chris spent his time reading the latest Nick Thacker pulp, but found himself often distracted. *It could just be that Jackie messed up—everyone does now and then*, he thought. But really, he knew it was because his friend's sharp mind was fading, along with his health.

The two of them didn't speak to each other again for the rest of the journey, even when the wild coast of Ireland appeared on the horizon and distant cranes pointed the way in. But on the morning they were due to dock, Chris found an envelope taped to his locker. Inside were 500 euros and a note saying "best of luck."

An hour later, he was standing on deck in the shadow of vast shipping containers. As an icy wind whipped across the deck, a member of the crew approached him, nodded at him without a word, and clanked open the door of one of the containers.

Chris stepped into the dark box, the smell of gasoline hitting him immediately as the door slammed closed behind him. One of the crew who was about the same size as Chris had donated some sturdy blue jeans and a black leather jacket which he was now wearing, but they were failing to keep out the freezing cold.

As his eyes adjusted to the dark, he could see there was a single car in the container, up against the back wall with very little space at either side. He tried the driver side door and it opened. He squeezed into the driver's seat, gently pulled the door closed, and sank into a leather seat that was the only comfortable thing about his situation. Then, he waited.

After more than an hour, a loud bang alerted him to the fact that something was happening. The container was suddenly rocking, and he gripped the steering wheel to keep himself steady. He could feel the container being lifted into the air, swaying and twisting. Finally, it clanked down hard onto the back of a truck.

As the truck's engine started up, Chris's heart rate quickened. He needed some good fortune. If this was Dover in England, or Calais in France—where cross-channel people smuggling was rife—his chances of being detected would be very high. He knew Irish customs wouldn't check every container, but he had to hope they didn't have the heart-beat monitors and other sophisticated detection equipment found in places with high levels of people smuggling.

Through the metal walls he could hear voices, and he listened carefully for anything coming closer. The truck was rolling slowly along, and it was difficult to judge how close the sounds were.

Come on, he said quietly, willing the truck to start moving faster and let him know he was clear. But instead, it slowed down ... then rolled to a stop. He was listening for clues as to what was happening when the bolt on the container began to creak. Then the door banged open and was immediately followed by the sound of a dog barking, the deafening noise echoing around the walls of the container.

13

A VAGUE PROFILE

The sultry heat of Yangon clung to Tsu as she walked close to the river in the south of the city. There was only one jazz club in this part of town, and she wanted to find it. She made her way past small shops blasting out painfully high-pitched pop music, before laying eyes on the building she was looking for.

The Sofaer building was easy to spot. Built in the early years of the twentieth century, its facade with tall columns topped by gargoyles and ornate stone carvings was dirty yet grand. Inside was the Aria jazz club, where Tsu hoped to find Nabyr, or at least something that might lead her to him.

She had recently learned that he was likely Indian, but beyond that she knew very little about him. What she did know, though, was that he liked to indulge. He was young, making money, and enjoying his new-found wealth. An asset—who'd heard Nabyr's name mentioned in association with a known arms dealer—had told Tsu his debauchery was what he was most notable for.

Tsu walked into the club and felt immediately out of place. She could see round tables set up in front of the stage, and a band playing a slow tune that glided through the room at the same lazy pace as the rising cigarette smoke. All of the tables were filled by men, and the only women in the place were serving drinks.

Blending in wouldn't be easy, but there was no way she was leaving. She strode up to the bar and ordered a Scotch. Then she took a seat at the back of the room ... and watched.

For the next hour, she observed the presence on stage switch between the all-male jazz band and groups of seven or eight women, who swayed gently to the music and occasionally spun around. If this was dancing, they were making little effort with it. It was clear they were just displaying themselves for the onlookers, who might choose them for whatever sordid purpose they had in mind.

Tsu had seen nobody fitting Nabyr's vague profile: an Indian who liked to overindulge. But it was far too early to rule out that this was his place. She went back to the bar and waited to order another drink.

"Cognac!" a voice shouted behind her as a finger and thumb clicked loudly close to her ear. She turned to see the back of a man as he walked towards a door marked "VIP." She twigged that he had mistaken her for a waitress and acted fast.

She walked down the bar to where the bartender was finishing up serving someone.

"Hey!" she told him. "The bathroom is disgusting, someone needs to deal with it. Now!"

"Yes, madam," the barman said, hurrying off from behind the bar. Tsu reached over the bar and grabbed a bottle of cognac, picking up a tray as she moved away.

She headed towards the door the guy who'd given her orders had walked through. She opened it and stepped confidently in. Waitresses in this situation would not be expected to speak, and she knew it. She would be expected to put down the drinks and leave quickly.

She set the cognac down on the table, which she noticed had scattered white powder on its black surface. As she stood, she glanced briefly at the face of the man sitting on a plush velvet sofa beside a glamorously dressed woman who was staring at him adoringly. She was likely Burmese, and he appeared to be Indian.

"Ya!" the man shouted as Tsu was leaving. "Glasses!" She ignored him.

She darted quickly out of the club and around a corner, staying nearby but out of sight. Luckily, the thing she was looking for right now was the one thing Yangon had plenty of. Scooters. Three men were standing around theirs on the opposite corner of the street, chatting and smoking.

Tsu walked up to them and spoke in Burmese. It wasn't a language she was fluent in, but she managed to tell them what she wanted: to loan one of the scooters and a helmet for a few hours in exchange for a handful of notes. Waving around the equivalent of three days' wages seemed to get what she wanted more effectively than her broken Burmese.

After waiting for two hours in the still, oppressive heat, she saw Nabyr and his female companion walking out of the club. The door to a black BMW was opened for him and he ducked inside. Tsu waited until the car started up and rolled a short distance away, then got the scooter's engine working.

Obscured by the helmet and with significant traffic around even late at night, she was able to follow Nabyr unnoticed as he headed north towards the city's more affluent suburbs. After twenty minutes, she saw his car turn onto a quiet residential street and pull to a stop outside an impressive mansion. She drove past and out of the street, before stopping around the corner and waiting.

This was a difficult one to judge. She knew alcohol wasn't the only intoxicant Nabyr had imbibed, and she also knew that with his female companion joining him he wouldn't likely be going to sleep any time soon. Playing it safe, she waited on the dark, quiet street for two more hours. Waiting was something she was used to.

Finally, she stepped stealthily towards the mansion and looked for signs of activity. There weren't any, but there didn't seem to be an easy way in either.

She walked as lightly as she could across the driveway and down the darkest side of the house. She pinned herself to the wall as she looked for a way in. She found a side door and slowly twisted the handle. It was locked. She crept further along the wall until she reached the back of the house. Looking up to her left, she noticed a small window that was slightly open.

It occurred to her that often forgetting to eat might help her out in this case, and figured she might just be able to squeeze through. She jumped up and deftly grabbed the window ledge, pulling herself up before prizing the window open as far as she could. She squeezed herself through the opening, trying not to make a sound as the window frame cut into her body. She dropped to the floor on the other side and allowed her eyes to adjust.

She was in an opulent hallway lined with huge vases on both sides. She noticed the strong smell of incense as she walked across an exquisite rug towards a door that was ajar. She could see there were no lights on in the next room, and she gently pushed opened the door to a lounge. She made her way through the mansion's ground floor rooms, looking for drawers, desks, anywhere that people leave documents.

She found herself in a small study with a wooden desk in the corner topped by a computer. She pushed the computer's power button and a few seconds later the password screen flashed up. Hacking was not her area of expertise, so she abandoned that option and switched off the computer to get rid of the light that might attract attention.

She looked down and pulled open the desk drawers one by one. Most were filled with cigar paraphernalia, but in a bottom drawer her eyes landed on an envelope that had already been opened. She picked it up and pulled out what she quickly realized were airline tickets. A flight to Bamako, Mali, three days from now in the name of Nabyr Barooah.

She made a mental note of the flight details, and was putting the envelope back when she heard a noise. A woman. Pleasure. *Sounds like fake pleasure,* Tsu couldn't help thinking to herself, *but either way it means people are awake.*

She turned, slipped out of the study and began making her way out. But the moaning was getting louder. There was no doubt they were coming closer, which was odd. She looked around, deciding if it was best to use the window again or try to unlock a door from the inside. The screaming was quickly becoming even louder, and she turned to see two entwined bodies on the staircase. She was looking at Nabyr's naked back and the woman's face hanging over his shoulder.

The woman's expression of ecstasy fell away as she looked into Tsu's face. She paused briefly, then let out an almighty scream. This one was not a scream of pleasure. Nabyr dropped her to the ground and spun around, his eyes wide. Tsu was turning to run as Nabyr jumped from the middle of the staircase to the bottom in one move, bouncing once and landing on Tsu's back.

She could feel his sweaty arm around her neck, squeezing her windpipe. She could hear him growling in her ear as he squeezed hard. She closed her eyes and threw all her weight forward, mustering just enough strength to bring him over her shoulder and send him flying into a vase. The beautiful ornament shattered into a thousand pieces as he crashed to the ground.

Tsu sprinted down the hallway to where there was a huge door that she prayed would let her out of the house. If she could find the lock. She could hear bare footsteps thudding down the hallway towards her. Her eyes searched in the darkness for a latch or bolt that would open the door. Nabyr was right behind her as she found the lock. She twisted it and pulled open the door, then darted out and slammed the door behind her as Nabyr's fingers were gripping on to it.

She didn't look back to see if Nabyr had chosen to chase her naked into the night. She just sprinted to her scooter, jumped on, and sped away.

14

SPOOKS IN GRAVEYARDS

As the sound of the dog's relentless barking hammered into his ears, Chris tried to make a quick decision. If he ran, he knew it was very unlikely he would get far. If he waited, he would surely be caught. He decided he couldn't just sit there and await his fate. He visualized what he was about to take on. If the dog got a hold of him, he knew the best thing to do would be to break its ribs—a dog's weak spot. But he was banking on the slim chance he could somehow swerve the dog and get running before anyone could catch him.

Then, the barking suddenly stopped.

"Heel!" somebody shouted at the dog. "Heel!"

Chris listened hard to pick up what voices just outside the container were saying.

"I'll have to get a team in here," someone with an Irish accent said. "If the dog is making a noise like that, we have no choice but to check it out."

"There's nothing in there—only the car I have documents for," someone with a French accent replied.

"That might be true, but as far as I know there could be, drugs, explosives, anything. So if you'll kindly follow me, sir, we'll let a team have a look then you can be on your way."

"This must be a joke …," Chris heard the French voice say, but it was getting quieter. He had to gamble that they were moving away. He slipped out of the car, and in a crouch stepped softly towards the container door. Very slowly, he pushed it open and peeked outside. He was in a line of trucks waiting to pass through a barrier and out into Ireland.

He couldn't see anybody in the immediate area, so he jumped as lightly as he could out of the container and moved quickly away, keeping low and darting among the trucks. He knew that trying doors to find one that was open would take too long. He was looking for a truck with a high ground clearance, and something solid to hold onto in its undercarriage. He hadn't done this kind of thing for years, but he was going to have to get used to dangerous situations again. Fast.

After a few minutes he found a truck that looked vaguely suitable and wasted no time, sliding through the dirt underneath the truck and looking for something solid to grip. He grasped hold of warm metal with both hands, swinging his legs up and jamming his toes between pipes.

Even in the bitter cold, sweat was beginning to line his forehead as he gripped on.

Just … move, he thought, willing the truck to move off

and take him well away from the dock. Horns sounded around him, but the trucks stayed still. He clung on and waited.

Finally, the engine roared close to his ears and the truck started moving, kicking up stones around him. He gripped tight and closed his eyes, knowing that every passing meter could be one closer to freedom.

Suddenly, the truck picked up pace and the road became smoother. Wind was blasting past him and whipping his face, but that meant open road and he was confident he would soon be clear. He began mentally preparing himself for rolling out from under and sprinting away as soon as he could.

He had to wait for the right time, when the truck slowed down but there wasn't too much traffic around. His hands and face were covered in dirt and oil by the time the chance arrived. The truck slowed, he assumed for lights, and he couldn't hear any other traffic around. He peered through the gap between the truck and the road and saw a grass verge lining what looked like a field, and knew it may be the best chance he'd have.

He released his grip and thudded to the ground, landing on his back and immediately rolling towards the edge of the road. The engine roared up again before he was out, and the huge back tire rolled towards him, whizzing past his head. He made it out with only an inch to spare and slid down the grass verge, landing on his feet in a ditch. He ducked down to keep out of sight of the road, then allowed himself to catch his breath.

He looked around and saw he was in a rural area

which he calculated was southeast of Galway. He knew he needed to be further inland, a place called Caldare, where Ned's contact was due to meet him. He had no map and was relying on memory of the one he'd looked at a few days earlier. He figured that even if he could find the place easily enough, it would be a three-hour walk. He wiped his hands on the cold, wet grass in front of him, then stepped out of the ditch and began walking.

He made his way through winding country lanes flanked by barren fields and walls built from rough limestone. Light was fading when he saw what he hoped was the village appearing on the horizon.

Quaint stone houses greeted him as he walked into the tiny village, well aware that he looked out of place in his dirty clothes. Then again, he probably did look like the kind of guy who would hang around a graveyard, which is where he was heading to now.

The village's medieval church wasn't difficult to find, with its slightly crooked spire standing over the houses. He creaked open the moss-covered gate and trudged into the graveyard through long grass that creeped up around the headstones.

While he waited, he read some of the grave stones, many of which listed causes of death ranging from "died for the freedom of Ireland" to "fell off a roof."

"You often find spooks in graveyards," a voice said over his shoulder.

"How do you know I'm a spook?" Chris asked, turning around to look at the guy. He was tall, round, and had a pathetic attempt at a combover.

"I know your face, pal. But I'll give you the question anyway, so you know I'm your guy."

"I appreciate it."

"How many times did they rebuild the Chain Bridge? Whatever the fook that is."

"Seven," Chris said, smiling.

"Aye," the man confirmed. "Your man in D.C. said you wouldn't let that catch you out. Said you're a smart fella."

"If that's what an agency guy thinks passes for smart, that's worrying," Chris said.

Ned's contact motioned for Chris to follow him. The man introduced himself as Carl, then said:

"I've checked you in to a room at the pub. Everything you need is in a sealed package in the toilet cistern. I left you some clothes too. It looks—and smells—like you could do with a change."

"Thanks," Chris said. "The pub sounds a little too public for my liking though."

"Well, Ned managed to get you a safehouse in France, the details are in the package. But Galway proved a little more difficult. So it's the pub or the graveyard."

"I'm not sure if news of my alleged crimes will have reached Ireland, but I feel like the more sensible choice is the graveyard," Chris replied, only half joking.

"Don't worry," Carl told him. "I know everyone who ever drinks in the pub, and even if they do recognize you, they're not the types to contact law enforcement. In fact they avoid law enforcement like the plague. They are looking forward to seeing how much you can drink though."

"Great," Chris said sarcastically. "You couldn't organize a safehouse so you organized a party instead?"

"Impress 'em, and they'll make sure you're protected," Carl said, smiling.

"And what happens if I don't impress them?"

"We'll cross that bridge if we come to it …"

15

THE BIGGER THEY ARE…

I n the cozy bar of the Old Counting House pub, Chris looked down at the tray of drinks that had been plonked in front of him. Four pints of stout and eight large whiskeys—a round for four people. They'd had five rounds already.

The charming old pub had jagged stone walls, a roaring open fireplace, and photos hung haphazardly on the wall of drinkers who had frequented the pub throughout its history. But for Chris, the aesthetic appeal was quickly wearing off as the drinking became more and more gladiatorial. Chris and Carl had been joined by two men who seemed to be in their seventies but drank like they were in their twenties.

"Wait until Grizzly turns up," one of the men said. "He'll show us all how to drink."

"Yeah?" Chris said. "I thought we were drinking already."

"We're drinking," the man replied. "But you've never seen a man who can drink like Grizzly."

"What's his secret?" Chris asked.

"Practice."

"Got it."

"So, hey," the other older guy said to Chris. "Who's gonna be your next president?"

"I don't talk politics," Chris told him. "It doesn't end well."

"Ah, we're just chatting. No harm in it. I like that McGolden fella. He's one of the good guys."

Chris said nothing, and Carl threw him a look that said everything.

"McGoldrick," Chris corrected the old guy.

"Yeah, that's the chap. You like him?"

"As I said, I don't talk politics."

"Fine. What do you wanna talk about?"

Suddenly, the door to the pub was flung open, and a man filled the whole doorway. He had to duck as he entered the pub. He threw both arms open and roared. Almost his entire head was covered with hair, and only gleaming eyes and glowing red cheeks were visible between the hair and the beard.

"Grizzly!" one of the old men said, seemingly delighted.

The barman, grinning, handed Grizzly a full bottle of whiskey and no glass. The big man pulled off the top with his teeth and took a huge swig. Then he joined the others next to the fireplace.

"Who the hell is this?" he asked, looking at Chris.

"Our American friend," one of the old men told him.

"Can you drink, *friend*?" Grizzly asked.

"Not like you can, I've heard."

"You heard right. What work you in, *friend*?"

Chris noticed that Grizzly said the word "friend" with deliberate disdain.

"I'm out of work right now."

"Why's that?"

Grizzly was staring at Chris, who didn't like where this was going. He'd met plenty of people who dealt only in confrontation. That generally ended about as well as conversations about politics.

"Chris is ex-navy," Carl chipped in. "Your old man was a sailor too, right?" he said to Grizzly, trying to bring the conversation to a more cordial place.

"If he's ex-navy he should be able to drink. Not like the army guys can drink, but..."

Chris nodded and smiled.

"Are you ex-military yourself, sir?" he asked.

"Not quite. I don't much care for authority."

"Yeah? I think I'm beginning to understand that."

The next two hours were spent in much the same vein, the only difference being that Grizzly's aggressive comments became more slurred.

"How tall are you, *friend*?" Grizzly asked Chris, pointing at him and looking at him through one eye. Liquor had closed the other.

"6'5".

"I'm 6'7," Grizzly advised.

"Yeah? Good to know. What night's dick swinging night in this pub?" Chris asked.

"Funny," Grizzly said. "You're a funny guy." He slapped Chris on the shoulder, hard.

"Thanks. I'd appreciate it if you didn't put your hands on me though," Chris said. He was getting pretty sick of this guy.

"Oh, did I hurt you? Sorry," Grizzly said. Then he tapped the side of Chris's face twice, a fake comforting gesture that was just hard enough to hurt. Before he knew it, Chris's right hand was launching across the table. It landed below Grizzly's right eye, sending the big man falling back, his head bouncing off the carpet.

Chris stood as Grizzly shook off the blow, beginning to get his feet. Before Chris could get around the table, Grizzly was standing. On his way up, he picked up a stool and hurled it in Chris's direction, missing badly. It crashed through a window that made a violent noise as it shattered. Grizzly dived across the table, sending drinks scattering across the pub and crunching his shoulder into Chris's chest.

Chris was pinned against the wall and instinct kicked in. He wrestled with the big man, trying to move his huge body away from him. He shoved as hard as he could then forced Grizzly's head downwards as he brought a knee up under his chin, sending his head snapping back. Chris seized the chance, landing two heavy right hands. Grizzly's eyes rolled in his head, and Chris watched as his huge body fell like a tree.

One of the old guys went to help Grizzly, but Chris

got there first, hammering three more punches into his face as he lay on the ground. He stopped when he felt hands on his shoulders, pulling backwards. He could hear Carl's voice in his ear, bringing him back to his senses.

"Chris! Man, stop!" Chris got to his feet and looked down at Grizzly, bloodied and unconscious. As he tried to come to terms with the fact he had lost control, the door to the pub flew open and an elderly lady burst in.

"I'm fockin' sick of you fellas in this fockin' pub!" she shouted. "I've told you I don't know how many times before about the noise, so now the garda are comin'."

"Chris knew that the garda was the Irish police. And if they were on their way, then so was he. He ran upstairs to his room, grabbed the package from the cistern, then darted downstairs and out of the pub.

16

I, MUSTACHE

The monochrome deserts of Arabia lay thousands of feet below Tsu as she looked out of the plane window, the sheer expanse of the landscape helping to calm her thoughts. She was happy to have succeeded in getting a head start on Nabyr and, assuming he took the flight on the tickets she had seen, she would be in Bamako a day before him. That gave her time to prepare.

Her mind was less at ease with her decision to go to Bamako at all. She wondered if she should have tried to grab Nabyr while she was at his home.

He was a big guy and wouldn't have been easy to subdue. Plus, her government was not on friendly terms with Myanmar's rulers. Getting the local police involved or trying to somehow extradite Nabyr would not be easy.

But deep down she knew the main reason she had run instead of fighting was that she would have to have dealt with Nabyr's lover—probably take her out. She had missed an opportunity because of sensitivity for the potential collateral. She wondered if she was going soft.

Now, it was too late. She convinced herself that even if she had captured him, he wouldn't talk easily, and she would learn more by following him. She pledged to have more words with herself later about whether she really was losing her edge. She spent the rest of the flight listening to music and trying to be as serene as possible, knowing she wouldn't get the chance to be tranquil again for quite a while.

TWENTY-FOUR HOURS LATER, she was sitting in a rental car outside Bamako–Sénou International Airport, watching the arrivals exit. Her face was covered by a niqab, which in the predominantly Islamic country was a good way to blend in and hide her identity. Only her eyes were uncovered.

It was two hours after Nabyr's flight was supposed to land, and once again, Tsu was waiting. She watched person after person amble out of the airport surrounded by luggage, until finally the emergence of two burly men with earpieces alerted her to the fact that Nabyr may be about to exit. She suspected he had stepped up his personal security since she had gained entry to his home.

Shades covered Nabyr's face as he walked through the sliding doors, and even from a distance Tsu thought she could see a bruise peeking out from under the glasses.

Nabyr ducked into a waiting silver Audi A7 which moved away as soon as the door was closed.

Tsu turned the key and drove her car in the same direction, leaving a couple vehicles between herself and Nabyr's driver. She followed the car through tree-lined streets, the well-paved roads around the airport quickly turning to poorly-kept tracks full of potholes that made her vehicle shudder every few meters.

Colorful makeshift stalls of crooked wood frames and plastic sheets had been pitched up in the red dirt along the side of the road, and children approached the car waving fruit or cigarettes next to the window during regular bottlenecks of traffic.

Tsu had extensive knowledge of plenty of countries, but Mali was not one of them. From the quick reading up she had done on the plane, she figured they must be heading towards one of the upmarket residential areas of the city that sit south of the Niger river.

The problem with upscale areas, she was well aware, was that there is usually less traffic and fewer people around. That made it more difficult to blend in. An hour after they had left the airport, Nabyr's car was close to the river, with Tsu following a few vehicles behind.

They were clearly now in an affluent neighborhood, and Tsu kept a look out for signs they might be about to stop. Nabyr's car made a right down a street that had no other cars on it, and looked like it might even be a private road. She made a quick decision that it was too risky to follow and kept driving straight, looking over her shoulder at where Nabyr's driver had turned.

Just before the car disappeared from sight, she noticed it was slowing down outside a large modernist mansion with big black gates and barbed-wire topping the surrounding wall.

She hoped she had been right in thinking they were stopping there, and made a plan to go back later under cover of darkness. In the meantime, she needed to change her vehicle. She took back the hire car, which someone with Nabyr may or may not have spotted, and switched it for a scooter that might help her avoid the endless pot holes.

THAT THICK BARBED wire really takes the edge off the architecture, Tsu thought as she gazed at the streamlined white mansion through the darkness. Excitement that she might see some of Nabyr's associates come and go, or at least confirm Nabyr himself was in there, was being replaced by monotony and random thoughts that come and go during hours of waiting.

She was crouched behind bushes in a rock hard field fifty meters from the house, insects buzzing around her ears and sweat running down her neck.

I really thought I'd go out in a more glorious way than malarial infection, she thought to herself. It was getting close to midnight, and she engaged in a mental battle between feeling that she was wasting her time and feeling guilty for letting any kind of discomfort get the better of her.

Then, a decision was made for her. She ducked further down behind the bushes as headlights appeared on the road close to the mansion. Two more cars were following. They pulled up to the black gates, which slowly opened to reveal four security guards waving the cars in. All of the guards were all holding semi-automatic weapons. Clearly, Nabyr wasn't taking any chances after the home invasion in Yangon.

She watched the three cars drive in and the gates close behind. She was too far away to see any faces or plates.

Ten minutes later, she noticed lights towards the top of the mansion. A rooftop terrace was illuminated, and she could see the heads and shoulders of people emerging from the house. Then the music started. A relentless beat that wouldn't stop for the next six hours.

With insects and humidity besieging her from all around, she stayed in the field as the sound of fun and frivolity drifted across the night. She hated everyone at the party, and she had only ever laid eyes on one of them.

As the sun slowly came up in the huge African sky, adding new layers of sweat to her body, Tsu could hear that the party was finally winding down. She prayed that the waiting hadn't been in vain and that cars and people, more visible in the daylight, would emerge from the mansion.

Her patience was rewarded when the gates opened and vehicles began driving out. The windows were tinted and she couldn't see faces, but she memorized the plates.

Then, she kept low as she moved along the edge of the field towards her scooter. When the cars were sufficiently far away, she set off behind them.

Despite it still being early in the morning, the streets of central Bamako were crowded with cars and pedestrians, mixing together with seemingly no distinction between the road and the sidewalk. Such a melee was good for remaining obscured, but it made following vehicles difficult. Tsu managed to just keep the three cars in her sight until they reached the embassy district, at which point one of the vehicles went its own way.

She decided to follow the other two, and shortly afterwards they pulled into the expansive forecourt of The Statesman Hotel. Porters in ill-fitting top hats and tails came to meet the cars, and Tsu did her best to catch a glimpse of the people getting out.

A man and a woman emerged from one of the cars, keeping their backs to Tsu as they entered the hotel. She cursed her luck as she turned her gaze to the other car. A tall, thin man climbed out and turned to one of the porters, seemingly talking to him with some stern instructions. She could see half his face, just enough to make out a mustache. Then he span and walked into the hotel.

She parked her scooter haphazardly by the side of the road and strode towards the hotel. She wasn't going to let this chance go. She pulled her headscarf over as much of her face as possible, then entered the cool, calm lobby.

She scanned around for any sign of the man. She

glanced over at reception and then the elevators, but couldn't see anyone with his build. Then, she spotted him. A waitress was taking his order in the lobby lounge. Tsu thought coffee sounded great just about now.

She took a seat in the lounge a few tables away from the man, her face turned away from him and towards a large mirror through which she could get a good look at his face.

The black coffee she ordered was superb, and she savored its strong flavor while keeping an eye on Mustache. This was a much more appealing place to conduct surveillance than any she had been recently, and she was happy to wait to see if anyone would join the guy.

But soon, he had finished his coffee, and stood to leave. He headed towards the elevators and Tsu was tempted to follow, but her instincts told her it was too bold. Her heart sank as she realized what was needed. More waiting.

For the next two days, Tsu occupied a seat at a red plastic table outside a run-down barbecue restaurant across the street from the hotel. The owner was absolutely delighted that she seemed to like his food so much, and mercilessly kept bringing her more.

Meanwhile, she watched Mustache come and go. He always left the hotel alone and came back alone. Both evenings, he emerged immaculately dressed and stepped into a waiting car.

On the third and fourth days, Tsu followed him. But his days were unremarkable—jewelry shopping, a visit to a museum, and a round or two of golf. She followed him to the same restaurant both nights—a chic French joint with fountains on the leafy terrace and chandeliers visible through the windows. He met different women on the two different nights. On the fifth night, Tsu decided, the next woman would be her …

17

ON THE RUN

Chris shielded his eyes from the crisp morning sunlight as he stood in a quiet corner of Galway bus station. He had a scarf covering the bottom half of his face and a beanie hat on his head.

It was 06:30 in the morning and he was waiting for the first bus to Cork, four hours away on the other side of the country. The slow shuffle of early morning passengers matched Chris's own lethargy. He had grabbed a couple hours' freezing cold sleep in a bus shelter in the countryside between the village and the city, then made his way into central Galway before it got light. He wanted to spend as little time as possible with his face on view.

The bus pulled in on time and Chris got on board, making his way to the back and sinking into a window seat. He pulled the scarf up over his face, and slept.

He only awoke when the driver announced they were thirty minutes away from Cork. He looked out of the window at brown farmland hardened by frost. His body was aching from the scrap with Grizzly, but the sleep had done him good. He was ready to walk confidently through customs at Cork using the false passport Carl had given him.

He stepped off the bus and found a taxi.

"Man, I'm tired. Crossed the whole country," he said in an Irish accent when he got in. He asked the driver to take him to the ferry terminal, then he pulled the scarf over his face and pretended to sleep. Thirty minutes later, the sea breeze filled his lungs as he emerged from the cab and looked around.

It wasn't the biggest port in the world, but he would have to move around the place to find the ferry to Roscoff, France. He would be glad when he was on board and could find a quiet corner. Spending time with his face covered and his eyes closed was an ideal scenario all round right now.

But before then, he had to be slick. He had seen a garda vehicle within the first five minutes of being at the port. It wasn't surprising for there to be some kind of police presence around an international port, but he wanted to keep that presence as far away from him as possible.

He observed his surroundings surreptitiously as he headed for the terminal building. He cursed his luck when he saw three police officers on foot, standing on the pathway in front of him. He turned and looked for another way into the building. Across the parking lot, he saw another garda vehicle pulling up, full of officers.

His heart started beating harder. He told himself it

might just be paranoia, but this looked like too many police for normal port security operations. He scanned around for options. There was a small cafe on the edge of the parking lot, and that looked like a good way to get out of the open. He made a beeline for the cafe and walked in out of the cold, looking for the bathroom as soon as he entered. But the TV in the corner caught his eye.

Guarda search for American fugitive read the news ticker at the bottom of the screen. He tried to listen to the newsreader over the sound of chatter and boiling coffeemakers.

Potential presidential candidate Matthew McGoldrick told reporters he has asked law enforcement to make the case of the fugitive former CIA Deputy Director a priority, he heard the anchor saying.

Chris felt like his blood was running cold. He put his head down and headed out of the cafe, trying to maintain a normal walking pace. He kept away from the line of cars waiting to board ferries and headed to where trucks were parked up, their drivers likely asleep inside. He walked between the trucks at a quick but steady pace, making his way out of the port.

Without looking back, he followed the coast until the concrete of the docks disappeared and the landscape began to turn more green. He took the smallest roads possible, choosing country backroads overhung by trees. Traffic was mercifully quiet and the groups of whitewashed cottages that occasionally appeared along the road seemed empty in the middle of the day.

But even the sound of an engine made the hairs on

the back of his neck stand up, and the sound of distant sirens would have sent him close to panic if his training hadn't taught him how to deal with such levels of stress.

After three hours of walking he still hadn't come up with a plan. He guessed someone must have reported a sighting of him in Ireland. He needed to get out of the country, but that would be very difficult now. He knew the Republic of Ireland had some wild areas where he might hide out for a while, but it was no good as a long-term plan. Plus, he had to investigate Basem, and hopefully McGoldrick as a result. That was the only way to really get his freedom back.

He was running options through his head when he glanced up, and stopped dead in his tracks. There was a police roadblock dead ahead, 100 meters down the road. He immediately took a sidestep into the trees by the side of the road. He turned 180 and didn't look back. He was trudging through wet mud and fallen leaves when the sound of a siren started up behind him. It was so much louder than the ones he had heard earlier.

His walk became a run, and he stumbled on the uneven ground. He looked up at the sky, hoping it was close to nightfall. He figured sunset was at least an hour away. He plunged further into the woods until he found the thickest collection of trees he could. He crouched down, leant back against the thick trunk of on oak tree, and breathed hard.

18

I'M ON A BOAT

I cy wind was blowing off the sea and into the woods where Chris was now standing, whipping around tree trunks and rustling leaves. It made it harder to listen for footsteps, but Chris was sure he could hear the sound of heavy boots not far away.

The nearby sound of a dog barking confirmed what he feared—that the garda had followed him into the woods and were close. He moved off in the opposite direction to the noise, but he knew that direction would take him to the coast. He had to hope the coastline wouldn't leave him too exposed.

He pushed on through the woods as the trees gradually became less clustered and the sea breeze grew stronger. The sea's gray waves appeared before him in the distance, and he could see he was about to emerge onto very high cliffs. The clifftop was covered with long grass, but it wasn't enough to hide him.

It was a difficult choice to move out of the cover of

the trees, but he knew that if he stayed in the small woods too long he would eventually be found. He sprinted through the wet grass to the edge of the cliff and looked for a way down.

The cliffs were extremely steep, and wet from the wind that was sweeping in off the sea. Trying to climb down would be extremely dangerous, but in his desperate situation he found himself thinking that would be a good thing, because people less desperate than him were unlikely to ever attempt it.

He took a deep breath, sank to one knee, and let his other leg dangle over the edge of the cliff. He gripped onto the slippery rock as firmly as he could while he carefully lowered himself down. In the fading light, he looked for footholds and ledges, his fingers getting less dexterous as they became more and more cold.

He took long, steady breaths, trying with great difficulty to keep calm as he made his way down. He searched only for the next step, refusing to look up to the top of the cliff or all the way down to the sea.

He found a larger ledge than any he had seen near the top and thought it might give him a moment to rest. He put his right foot down onto it. He let the ledge take his weight while he tried to regain some energy. But the ledge gave way, crunching below his boot and shattering into several pieces as it fell towards the sea.

He grabbed out in panic at the first thing that came to hand, a small branch from a shrub growing on the rock face. But the branch was weak and he knew it wouldn't last long. The breaking rock had thrown him off balance and his feet searched wildly for something firm below him.

His feet kept slipping off the rock and he could feel the branch tearing away from the cliff. Fear was growing in his chest as he began to lose control. Then, he was falling.

He dropped through the air and could see only sky above him. He tried to keep himself upright but he was in free-fall. The impact when he landed was like being shot, and he could feel his arm was crushed beneath him … before the world went black.

CHRIS OPENED his eyes and saw the moon above him. A second later, the pain from his head and arm registered. He didn't know if he would be able to move. He pulled his torso upright as his head throbbed.

He could see he had landed on a large, flat rock maybe twenty meters above the sea. He staggered as he got to his feet. In a daze, he tried to formulate a plan. But the only plan he had right now was to keep moving. Anywhere.

He clambered across large rocks, grimacing when he put his injured arm out to stop a fall. He slowly made his way downwards towards the shore with only moonlight to show him the way.

Eventually, his boots sank into the rough sand where the waves were lapping onto the shoreline, and he noticed the smell of the sea that normally gave him such pleasure.

He looked ahead down the coast. He noticed what looked like small boats bobbing in the water, and stopped dead in his tracks. Any sign of humanity was not good.

But there were no lights on the boats, and he hoped nobody would be around at this hour. Then a thought crossed his mind. It was a thought that surprised him.

What if I take one?

Stealing something, and of all things someone's boat, was against his nature. At least, he thought it was. But he found he couldn't shake the idea. In fact, he realized it might be the only workable possibility he had.

He knew that small boats like that often had outboard motors that weren't protected by locks or codes. But he also knew that a boat with poor protection was likely a boat with poor equipment. One that wouldn't be well suited for the journey to northern France, which he estimated would be at least a twelve-hour sail.

But despite both the risk and the moral quandary, his mind was being quickly made up. As the boats got nearer, he hoped he would soon be on the waves. He reached the boats, gently bobbing on the moonlit water in the dead of night. His first priority was to find one that had an engine without any protection. Ideally, he also wanted one that offered a little bit of shelter.

He searched among the boats, treading carefully on the shingle beach and looking around for any signs of activity.

Finally, he found a boat that would make an acceptable candidate. From a short distance, the motor seemed to be unprotected, and there was a small cabin in which he could take shelter from the elements.

Minutes later he was on the boat, inspecting the engine. He realized he could start it up with ease. The fuel gauge was reading almost full, and there was a spare gas can in the cabin. There was no need to wait any longer.

Sorry, whoever you are. Hope you have insurance, he thought as the engine spluttered to life. Then he ducked into the cabin and began feeding the smooth wooden wheel through his hands, guiding the boat out onto the Celtic Sea.

19

MOJITO MEETING

At 11am, the cool, airy lobby of The Statesman was busy with people waiting to check out, and Tsu had picked her time carefully. The man she had been observing for the last few days always seemed to walk out of the hotel around late morning, and she gambled that he had a morning coffee or two before that.

At check-out time, she figured the lobby cafe should be busy enough that she might have to share somebody's table. She scanned the lobby lounge for signs of hair on a top lip, and felt her stomach tighten as she laid eyes on the man she wanted to get to know. She had to get into flirting mode fast.

She glided over towards him and was at his table before he looked up from his phone.

"Do you mind if I sit here?" she asked, looking around the room to show that the other tables were full. The man shrugged and said nothing.

She sat and ordered a coffee. She waited until it arrived, then started a conversation.

"Sorry to trouble you," she said. "But do you know how to get to the National Museum?"

The man seemed irritated, then looked at her face and his expression softened slightly.

"It's just a few blocks east," he told her in an accent she couldn't yet place. "You could easily walk there. But I don't suggest it."

"Thanks. What's wrong with walking, if you don't mind me asking?"

"It's filthy out there. And people will try to sell you whatever crap they're hawking as soon as you step foot out the door. It could be quite stressful for a woman alone."

"Ah. I see," Tsu replied. "Thanks for the advice. Well, I have been waiting days for my husband to show me around the city, but he's always too busy."

"Well, you're not missing much anyway," the man said.

"Oh, you've met my husband?" Tsu replied. The man suppressed a smile.

"I mean the museum," he said. "But I have no doubt that your husband doesn't deserve you."

"I tell myself he just has a lot on his plate. Anyway, thanks, and I'm sure I'll find something to do with the day."

The man finished the last of his coffee, threw a few notes on the table, and stood.

"Well, have a good day, whatever you end up doing," he told Tsu, then marched quickly off.

She shrugged off a fleeting feeling of inadequacy and told herself she couldn't always have it easy. It would just take a bit of time. She ordered another coffee and prepared herself to wait.

For the next six hours, the only place she went other than the hotel's cafe was a small store across the lobby. She chose the best book she could find among the shop's poor selection, then spent the rest of the day reading and waiting.

At 17:30, she saw Mustache walk back into the hotel. She discreetly stood and began walking across the lobby at an angle she judged would cross his path.

"Oh!" she said when she caught his eye. "How was your day?"

"It was fine."

"Well, I definitely made the right choice with mine. I took your advice and didn't brave the streets, so I ended up just sitting in the hotel bar and drinking mojitos."

Knowing the man would likely be parched after a day in Bamako's heat, her made-up choice of cocktail—crisp, minty and refreshing—was carefully chosen.

"That sounds like an excellent way to spend the day," the man said. "A mojito sounds very appealing right now."

"I could certainly take one more, too. How about meet me at the bar in an hour?"

The man paused as he looked at her.

"Aren't you going to meet your husband?"

" I have no idea where he is."

"I have an appointment this evening, but I should have time for one drink," the man explained.

"Perfect, see you soon."

AN HOUR LATER, Tsu was sitting in the corner of the hotel bar, the breeze from ceiling fans cooling her and blowing the large leaves of the many plants that decorated the bar. With its wicker furniture and white marble floor, the place was a picture of faded colonial grandeur.

It had been over an hour since she had 'bumped into' Mustache in the lobby. If she wasn't purely wooing him for his potential usefulness, she would already be tired of waiting for him.

Finally, dressed in an unpleasant light-blue suit, he showed up.

"Mojito?" he asked as the waitress came to take their order. He pointed at the glass Tsu had just finished.

"Actually, I've had enough of those today," she replied. I'll take a Scotch."

"Scotch it is," the man said, looking impressed.

"So did you do anything fun today?" Tsu asked. "Or something more productive than drinking?"

"Not really. I met a friend for lunch."

"Sounds relaxing at least. Do you know a lot of people in Bamako?"

"Not many. It's not my favorite city. I try to spend as little time here as possible.."

"I don't blame you. So what brings you here this time?"

"Just business."

Tsu didn't ask any other questions, she let silence force him to expand on his last answer.

"I'm in town for a meeting, but it's been pushed back. Unfortunately I might be here for another week or two."

"Unlucky for you. What kind of business are you in?"

"Nothing interesting, believe me."

"Okay, I believe you. So, where are you from originally?"

"North Africa. Morocco."

"Oh, that sounds nicer than Bamako! Which city?"

"Marrakech. And yes, it is nicer than Bamako. I'm in Mali quite often on business though."

"My husband's in Mali on business, too. Told me he'll be away for at least a week. Then he'll probably come back for a while, barely speak to me, and fly off somewhere again."

"Stories like that make me glad I never married."

"Probably a good move. But marriage does have its benefits. By the way, I'd appreciate it if you didn't tell anyone we spent time together. My husband would probably be upset, even if he doesn't seem to give a damn about me."

"Well, I should probably get going after this drink anyway."

"Sure. Are you going somewhere good for dinner?"

"Yes, as a matter of fact. A French place across town.

Not many good restaurants in this city but that one is actually superb."

"Really?" Tsu said enthusiastically, gazing into the man's eyes.

"Sorry, but I already have a companion for the evening. I'm not averse to a *ménage à trois* situation, but not quite this soon," the man said, smiling.

"Really!" Tsu said with even more enthusiasm.

"Yes, but that's a conversation for another day."

"I'll look forward to it," Tsu said as the man was standing to leave. "By the way, I didn't get your name."

"Osman."

"Lisa," Tsu said. "Pleased to meet you."

"Sorry to leave you alone, but as I said, I have an appointment."

"No problem. I'll walk out with you, I'm going to the barbecue place across the street."

Tsu walked with Osman over to reception and hovered a few meters behind him as he handed in his key. She was just close enough to see the room number written on the fob.

"Have a relaxing evening," Osman said as he walked out of the hotel.

It won't be relaxing, Tsu thought, *but it will be interesting.*

20

MURKY WATER

A drenaline was masking the pain of Chris's injuries as the boat he had stolen picked up speed and moved away from the Irish coast.

He knew he had a few things in his favor. His sailing knowledge, the fact that it was a clear enough night that he could use the stars to help with navigation, and the fact that it didn't matter which part of the French coast he landed on as long as there weren't too many people around.

But there were disadvantages, too. Big ones. This boat clearly wasn't made for such long journeys even if it was in great shape, and he had no idea what kind of shape it was in. He also didn't know for sure that the fuel gauge was working correctly.

He set the boat in a southeasterly direction, knowing from his years of poring over nautical maps that it would be open water so long as he avoided the south coast of

England. If he could be without view of any country's coastline before the sun rose, he would be happy.

He held the wheel with one hand and looked around the tiny cabin. Food would be good, and fresh water would be even better. He knew that either was probably too much to hope for. He saw no sign of any food, but he did see a plastic bottle that seemed to be full.

He reached down and picked it up, an unidentifiable slime making it slip in his fingers. The bottle was filthy. In fact, everything around him was filthy. He was dreading finding out just how old and out of shape this boat was when the sun rose.

He held up the bottle in front of his eyes and wiped away some of the grease. He twisted off the top and took a cautious sniff of the liquid. It didn't smell strongly of anything, and despite his stomach begging him not to, he took a swig. It was utterly disgusting.

It was water, he decided, and it was technically drinkable. But it was fresh water only in the sense of not being saltwater. It tasted like a combination of gasoline and fish, and there were tiny lumps of matter floating in it.

He swallowed as much as he could stomach, then shaking his head he put the cap back on. Waves never made him feel nauseated, but concussion combined with the repulsive drink sure did the trick.

It was around four hours into the journey when Chris thought he could see the lights of the British coast on his port side. They were far away, and he assessed he had done a decent job of staying away from the coastline.

But that success aside, his spirits were fading. His situation was taking its toll physically and emotionally. He hadn't been able to speak to his wife in over two weeks. And he was starting to think that investigating McGoldrick—and clearing his own name—would be impossible if all he could ever do was try to avoid arrest.

Then, he looked out at the ocean, thought about all the difficulties he had overcome before, and told himself to quit whining.

The sun was edging over the horizon, and the only life he could see were the sea birds circling overhead. For just a moment, he felt at peace. He looked ahead in the direction of France, but he knew it would still be hours before the coast appeared. He tried to plan how he might get ashore without being noticed, and wondered if he might have to wait until night fell again.

He was running options through his head when he turned around to inspect the boat—the first time he had been able to look at it in any kind of light. What he saw was a vessel no man should ever take to sea.

The metal was completely rusted, and the wood was close to rotting. Among the fishing nets and buoys were random objects that people had clearly thrown into the boat as if it were a skip: an old barbecue, a bicycle wheel, even a child's doll.

But worse than that—much worse—were the holes. He could see there were already two inches of water on the deck. He realized it must be coming in slowly through tiny holes or gaps where the wood had warped or rotted. He suspected the bilge pump would be in equally terrible condition and unable to cope with the water that was building up.

The one and only question Chris had in his mind right now was whether it would build up enough to sink the boat before he got to dry land. He knew that the problem would get worse more quickly as time went on, because the weight of the water on the deck would put the boat lower in the water, exposing more holes.

He looked up at the sky. In northern Europe at this time of year, he was aware that rain was always likely. It could come at any time. The sky was a mix of blue patches, high clouds, and lower gray clouds. Typical of a sky where the weather could change in seconds.

He searched the boat for something to start bailing out water. There was nothing of much use, not even a bucket. He felt panic rising in his chest. He picked up the old barbecue and ripped the grill off it, making a receptacle for the water. He began tipping over the side, and for the next hour he fought a losing battle. Then, the rain came.

It fell hard and heavy, and visibility was severely reduced. His situation was becoming desperate. He could see the sea getting higher and more water rained or leaked onto the deck. He tried to stay positive, but he also had to face the reality that sinking was now the most likely outcome.

He looked around for a lifebelt, but he knew it was useless. The boat didn't have even the basics. He didn't allow himself time to think about karma.

As he was looking up at the sky for the hundredth

time, praying to see clearing, he felt the boat tip sharply to one side. He looked at the edge that had tipped nearest to the water, watching as the sea began pouring over the starboard side. He tried to move to the port side and balance out the boat with his weight, but it was too late. The boat was capsizing.

He reached out for something, anything, to grab on to. But water crashed into his legs and took his feet from under him.

The shock of the icy water hit him as he plunged into the sea, seconds before the panic of being disoriented underwater kicked in. It doesn't matter how many years you have spent at sea, everybody panics in that situation.

It was dark and he knew the boat must be on top of him. He pushed his arms out in front of him and tried to swim out from under it. But his legs didn't follow. He tried again with a harder stroke, but he wasn't going anywhere. He could feel his left leg was caught.

He looked around and saw his leg was entangled in a fishing net. He tried time and again to pull his leg out, but it wouldn't move.

His panic was growing worse with every second he went without oxygen. He tried to reach the net with his hands, but it was just too far. Then, he realized he could reach his laces. Just. With freezing cold hands he pulled at the laces, trying to untie or loosen them enough to allow him to pull his foot out of his boot.

He twisted and pulled, his movements making the water murkier and obscuring his view. But he could tell the laces weren't getting looser.

Now, he was in total panic, trying to pull at the laces with a hand that was too numb to know if he was even holding them. He began yanking his leg towards himself again. It still wouldn't free itself, and he felt his last chance had gone. He paused briefly before frantically moving his leg, twisting and pulling it every way he could. It came loose, then was free.

Almost in disbelief, he immediately turned and swam. He moved past the edge of the boat and shot out of the water, opening his mouth to draw in air as he looked towards the sky.

Life rushed back into his body as the oxygen filled his lungs. But his mind turned sharply to the next problem. He knew that hypothermia would come fast ...

21

SEEMINGLY ALONE

Back in the lobby cafe and now sick of the sight of the place, Tsu sat and watched the reception of the hotel. She was waiting for a change of staff, hoping the woman Osman had handed his room key to would disappear off for a break.

It had already been an hour since Osman had left to go for dinner, and Tsu was getting twitchy. The more time that passed before she could get her hands on that key, the more risky it would be to try to get into his room. She figured in an old hotel like this the locks would be quite easy to pick, but doing so without getting spotted would be much less easy.

There was another way into his room, but that was an absolute last resort. For now, getting in there without his company was very much the preference.

Then, she got some luck. The woman on reception handed over to a man, a guy she hadn't seen there that evening. Earlier in the day, she had noticed an obscure exit out of the hotel down in the basement near the gym. She headed down there, slipped out of the side door onto the street, and walked around to the main entrance of the hotel.

She strolled in as if returning from dinner and walked up to the reception.

"326," she said, smiling at the guy. He smiled back before turning to pick the key off the wall behind him.

"There you go, madam," he said, handing her the chunky key. She thanked him and strolled towards the elevator, smiling at how easy that had been.

Once she was up on the third floor, adrenaline was kicking in. She unlocked the door, after having a quick check down the corridor to see if anyone would spot her going in. It was all quiet.

She walked into the room and noticed how pristine everything was. Osman's suits were lined up with matching shirts and ties ready to go, and three pairs of shoes were placed in a neat row beneath them. A pile of papers on the desk was stacked absolutely perfectly. She would have to be careful to put everything back just as it was.

She started with the suit pockets. They were empty except for the inside pocket of one jacket, which had the business card for a hotel and golf course in Marrakesh. The stack of papers on the desk turned out to be a brochure for a high-end golf course in Rabat, along with an itinerary for a "celebrity golf tour."

Does this guy do anything but play golf? Tsu thought to herself.

She checked the drawers and found nothing belonging to Osman, just the usual room service menus and hotel literature. She couldn't see any laptop or other electronics, and a search of his suitcase revealed only neatly folded shirts, underwear, and, of course, golfing gear.

She shrugged off momentary disappointment, because she hadn't expected him to leave anything incriminating lying around. Her priority was to hear things he might say when nobody was listening.

It could be that the guy was completely sweet and innocent, but if he was an associate of Nabyr—a man who traded illegal arms and ordered the assassination of her partner in Yangon—she found that extremely unlikely.

She stood on the bed and reached up above her head, twisting off the cover of the smoke alarm. She slipped a tiny device inside and quickly replaced the cover. After stepping off the bed, she smoothed out the covers to remove any trace that someone had touched them.

She was about to head for the door, when she decided to quickly flip the pillows over. Hiding confidential documents under pillows wasn't something she'd known anyone with any skill to do in the past, but the perfectionist in her made her want to check every inch of the room.

She flipped over the closest pillow. There were no documents underneath it, but there was certainly something. It took her a few seconds to register what she was seeing.

A mask of thick, black rubber, the partially folded eye and mouth holes giving the rubber face a grotesque expression. She neither wanted or needed to touch the mask. But it had given her very useful info. Clearly, this guy was into something other than golf.

She put the pillow back in place and slipped out of the room. She quietly closed the door, headed downstairs, and handed the key back to reception.

In the tiny apartment she had rented in Bamako, Tsu listened. It was 2am, and she had heard Osman return from dinner, seemingly alone.

Must be finding it difficult to meet a woman who's into what he's into, she thought.

Osman was whistling to himself and muttering a few sentences in Arabic. Tsu didn't know what he was saying, but it sounded like he was simply talking to himself in the way a lot of people do when they're alone.

Soon, she heard snoring. Loud, merciless snoring. She knew that he might have business with people from different time zones and could potentially receive a call at any time. But after two hours of snoring, she took pity on herself and allowed herself a couple hours' sleep.

At first light, she was listening again. Osman seemed to be up and about. Either that, or he was whistling in his sleep. Then, his phone rang.

Tsu sat up straight in her chair and pushed the earpiece further into her ear.

"Yes?" Osman said in English.

His conversation involved several references to "the American", and a couple to "the gathering." Tsu wondered if the discussion might simply be about a golf meeting, until one line made her sure it was not.

"It's quite simple," Osman told the person on the phone. "The American's job is to get the right people into that room. Our job is to make sure they don't get out alive."

22

FIRE IN THE SKY

I n the bitter cold of the Celtic Sea, Chris clung to his upturned boat. Most of his body was in the freezing water, and he was drifting in and out of consciousness. His breathing was slow and shallow, and in a rare moment of lucidity he knew he was in the latter stages of hypothermia.

He had tried to right the capsized boat, but the vessel was too large. Trying to turn it had taken too much energy, and now he barely had enough to cling on.

He tried to fight off another bout of unconsciousness, but his strength failed him, and the world went dark.

FIRE WAS BURNING away Chris's skin, destroying every part of his body. The terror was so bad he thought he must be in hell. The pain only increased and the flames engulfed him. He wondered why he wasn't dead. Suddenly, he opened his eyes.

Above him were two faces. The kinds of faces he had seen many times before: weathered by the sea.

"*Vivant!*" one of the men exclaimed, amazed that Chris was alive. The other man nodded solemnly as if more impressed than happy.

Chris could still feel his whole body burning, and realized all of his nerve endings were recovering from being in the cold sea.

Familiar rocking movements told him he was on a boat. He looked around the small cabin he had found himself in. It was clearly a fishing boat, not in great shape but a million times better than the one he had tried to sail from Ireland.

The unsmiling man brought over a cup of water and held it to Chris's lips. He raised his head and drank in as much as he could before exhaustion forced him to thud his head back onto the cushion beneath. He closed his eyes.

He opened them again when he felt somebody trying to lift him. He felt nowhere near well enough to move, but a man—a new face—insisted he get up. He put his feet on the floor, and felt sure his trembling legs wouldn't allow him to stand.

With the help of the fisherman, he slowly got to his feet. The man put a thick jacket around him and led him out of the cabin.

He squinted, his eyes almost closed as he emerged into bright sunlight. He was in a small harbor, with crooked, colorful buildings lining the shore. A few fishermen were lugging catches onto the beach, but there were no other people around.

"*Médecin?*," the fisherman said to him. "Doctor?"

Chris shook his head.

"No," he croaked. And then, more loudly, "no doctors."

"*Vin?*"

"No," Chris replied again. "No wine and no doctors."

The man shrugged and led him across the beach between large boulders and patches of seaweed. They walked a short distance through a small village, then turned onto a narrow cobbled street. Outside a bright yellow house, the man stopped and opened the door.

Inside the house, the man helped Chris up a flight of wooden stairs and into a room that for the last few days would have been beyond Chris's wildest dreams. A bedroom with a soft bed and the temperature just perfect. The fisherman gestured at the bed, then closed the door and left.

For the next two days, Chris slept.

Occasionally, the smell of freshly baked bread and strong coffee pierced his consciousness. He rolled over to see food and coffee had been left next to his bed, but despite the wonderful smell, he couldn't face them.

On the third day, he told his aching muscles to allow him to sit up, and he drank some of the coffee. It was cold and had obviously been left there hours earlier, but it was still one of the best things he had ever tasted. Bitter, deep, and life affirming.

Five days after he had landed in France, he pulled himself out of bed and walked down the wooden stairs, hoping to find his hosts and thank them for everything they had done.

It was early evening, and he could hear voices chattering. He reached the bottom of the stairs and walked into a kitchen. The windows were misted up with aromatic steam from a pot that was boiling away on the stove.

From the kitchen table, the faces of two men and two women turned towards him, and smiles crossed all of their faces.

"*Très bon!*" one of the women exclaimed, and pulled out a chair for him to join them. She pulled out a wine glass from the cabinet beside her, then glugged in red wine from an unlabeled bottle on the table.

Please one day let me meet someone teetotal, Chris thought as she handed him the glass. Then he checked himself for his lack of gratitude, and drank.

CHRIS COULD HAVE SPENT weeks in the cottage, being given wine and incredible food and being pressured into no conversation other than discussing which meals and wine were his particular favorites. But the strength he had regained might even be undone by overindulgence. And he had things to do.

On a crisp and clear morning, he was standing at a rural train station. The fisherman had paid for the train ticket with a fifty euro note then handed Chris the change.

Having said their goodbyes, Chris boarded a train bound for Bordeaux. He had lost what little he had when the boat sank—the false passports, his money, and everything else Carl had put in the package to help him.

But as he stared out of the window at the French countryside, he knew he had lost more than that. His reputation, his freedom, maybe even his moral compass. For now, he had even lost the ability to contact his wife. It was too risky. The only things he had gained were scars and an unkempt beard.

23

WHAT'S THE CONNECTION?

"You again," Osman said, smiling as Tsu walked up to his table in the lobby cafe. She needed to take things out of this place before people started to twig she was hanging around the cafe and bar but not actually staying at the hotel.

"Me again! Mind if I join you?"

Osman held out an open palm, gesturing for Tsu to sit.

"I've got nothing to do but hang around this hotel, so as long as you're staying here, you'll have to get used to bumping into me."

"I can get used to it."

Tsu smiled and hoped the guy was warming to her.

"The sad thing is, I usually like getting out and doing things. I like the outdoors. But in Bamako, getting outdoors just means pollution and hassle."

"There are a few green spaces in this city," Osman said. "Not many though."

"Yeah, like where? I can't say I've seen any."

"Well, I get some semi-fresh air on the golf course."

"Really? That sounds like a good way to get some semi-fresh air. I've never played, but I'd like to try some day."

"How about today?" Osman asked. Tsu smiled like it was a crazy idea.

"I guess so!" she said. "I'm sure I'll be terrible, but it sounds like fun!"

Two hours later, they were on the first hole at The Riverside Golf Club, getting ready to tee-off from a green mat that covered the brown, patchy grass of the course. There was no river in sight.

"Do you mind?" Osman asked as he moved towards Tsu, offering to show her how to swing. He placed his hand on her left arm to make sure she kept it straight, then touched the top of her hips to gently move her into the correct position.

She took her first swing, making sure to hammer the ball with a solid whack while sending it in the wrong direction. Feisty but willing to be led, that was the image she wanted to give, and she did so for the next three hours.

"Any news on your meeting?" she asked as they approached the ninth. "And getting out of Bamako?"

"I'm hoping middle of next week," Osman told her. "Then I can get out of Bamako and on to the next shithole."

"Oh wow!" Tsu said as she lined up to shank a drive into the leafless trees. "Sounds like you don't enjoy your work!"

"It is what it is."

"But you won't tell me what it is?" Tsu said, smiling playfully.

"Trust me, it will only bore you."

"Okay," she said, knowing when not to push too hard. "My husband is always boring me with his work complaints. When he's around to bore me at all. So if you want to talk about something more interesting, that's fine with me."

"What do you want to know?" Osman asked, desperate as all men are to rise to the challenge of being interesting.

"What do you do for fun?"

"This!"

"I mean real fun. You don't go to parties? Bars, clubs?"

"I do. Sometimes."

"Well, if you have any plans any time soon, I'd love you forever if you save me from another night of killing time alone."

Osman said nothing as he lined up his shot. He hit an unusually poor drive, then cautiously said:

"Well … I am going to a party on Saturday. It will be a little … crazy, though."

"That sounds perfect! What kind of crazy?"

"Let's just say some of the people I know are into

some pretty wild things. But you don't have to get involved. You can just enjoy the free drinks."

"Okay. That certainly sounds intriguing. What should I wear to a crazy party?"

"We usually like to have some kind of theme. I don't think it's been decided yet though."

Tsu lined up another drive, swaying her hips slowly as she found her position.

"I remember going to a masquerade ball a few years ago," she said. "I know that's not all that crazy, but it did make me feel kind of … sexy, you know?"

"I certainly do know," Osman said. "I'm sure they wouldn't be opposed to that suggestion at all."

AT 9PM ON SATURDAY NIGHT, Tsu stepped out of The Statesmen Hotel in a figure-hugging black dress that extended down to her ankles and had a large slit up one side, hinting at the flesh beneath. A sparkling mask was covering her face. The door to a Mercedes-Benz S-Class was opened for her and she ducked into the car, where Osman was already waiting.

"You don't need to wear your mask just yet," he told her.

"I love this thing," she said. "I want to wear it for as long as possible. Here, put yours on."

She picked up Osman's mask from his lap and slipped into onto his face before running her palm slowly down his cheek.

As they drove towards what she hoped would be

Nabyr's mansion, she caught the driver occasionally eyeing her in the mirror, and was glad she had put the mask on early.

With the direction they were heading, she was soon confident she would be attending Nabyr's party. Her heart and stomach were fluttering, but she remained the picture of calm.

They approached the modernist mansion and Tsu saw the field where she had spent so many miserable hours a few days earlier. The car drove up to the huge gates, which opened to reveal a guard on either side of the driveway, each holding a machine gun.

Outside the sliding glass doorway to the house, they stepped out of the car and were handed champagne from a tray held by a woman wearing a tiny gold bikini. Tsu took a sip, the top of the glass touching the bottom of the mask that rested just above her mouth.

They walked down a path that was lit by torches with open flames, and into a giant living space with immaculate white-on-white decor. Huge contemporary sculptures were dotted around the room. On one side, an entire wall was a fountain, and a clearly inebriated woman was dancing in it and laughing, the water falling into her champagne glass.

"Just enjoy yourself and mingle," Osman told Tsu. "I'll catch up with you later."

Tsu clinked his glass and went off to mingle. But it turned out that wasn't so easy. Nobody seemed interested in talking. They just looked her up and down through their masks, and spent their time imbibing as many substances as they could, whether it was the endless champagne or the white lines that appeared and quickly disappeared. Even the extravagant sculptures were fair game for racking up a line so long as they had a flat surface.

As the night went on, Tsu noticed that more of the guests were indulging in a different kind of pleasure. They were locked in passionate embraces, and engaged in acts that would normally be done in private.

More and more items of clothing were being discarded, and she hoped the masks wouldn't be discarded too. It would be useful to see the faces of some of the people at the party, but it was more important that her own stayed on. Nabyr had likely seen her face at least once, in the jazz club back in Yangon, and possibly again during the scuffle in his home.

She had seen little of Nabyr all evening. Once when he did appear, she saw him slap a waitress with the back of his hand for spilling a little champagne. He'd then grabbed the bottle and served it to guests himself, sloshing it around clumsily before it quickly ran out.

Osman was equally elusive. She guessed he was off enjoying everything the party had to offer, and would return to her later on when she was supposedly loosened up and ready to experiment.

After sipping a few drinks as slowly as she could get away with, she decided it was time to do what she was there to do. She'd noticed that through one of the doors was a hallway with a grand marble staircase.

Going upstairs to the bedrooms uninvited wouldn't

normally be party etiquette, but this was no normal party. On her way up the stairs, a woman passed her on her way down. She was naked except for the mask and, like the woman in the waterfall, was laughing maniacally to herself.

Tsu knew there would be a lot of rooms to search. Finding a study or master bedroom would be ideal. But the priority was to enter rooms with nobody in them. In that task, she had some help. She made the easy decision not to enter any room where ecstatic noises were coming from behind the door.

She made a guess that the master bedroom could be at the far end of the house, where she had spotted a large balcony on the second floor. She moved quickly to the end of the corridor, took a look to make sure nobody was around, and tried the door. It was locked. She put her ear to the door, but heard nothing.

She spotted a large window at the end of the corridor, and cautiously stuck her head out of it, looking in the direction of the balcony. It was unlit, and she took that as a sign that nobody was in the bedroom.

Beneath the window she could see a narrow ledge that extended all the way to the balcony. She looked down and saw that the garden below was dark and quiet. It would only take a few seconds to climb out of the window and shuffle along the stone ledge to the balcony. She thought she could do it without being spotted. The problem was how narrow the ledge was. Six inches wide at the most. And she was wearing heels.

She took off her shoes and tucked them behind a

plant in the corner of the corridor. She drew a deep breath as she clambered out of the window and lowered herself onto the tiny ledge. She began shuffling along, gripping on with only her toes. But her feet were slippery from sweating in the shoes and the humid night. She could see the balcony almost within arm's reach, but her feet were unsteady.

She reached out for the balcony and was about the grab it when her left foot slipped off the ledge, putting her off balance and out of control. She slipped from the ledge, her shins crashing into the wall as she flailed desperately.

She was already falling when she grabbed out at the bottom of the balcony. She wrapped her hand around a stone railing and managed to grip on, her legs dangling free below her.

She reached up with her other hand and got her fingertips onto the bottom of the balcony. By swinging her legs and using every ounce of strength in her arms, she heaved herself up. She climbed over the railings of the balcony, and breathed. Then she twisted the door handle, fearing all the effort would be for nothing. It opened.

She slipped inside the dark bedroom, deciding where to begin searching. The bedside cabinets revealed nothing but jewelry and beauty accessories. The closet was full of expensive clothes, men's suits for a man of Nabyr's size and feminine clothing for women of various sizes. Then, beneath the clothes, she saw a safe.

She bent down and saw it had a simple key lock

without the need for a digital code. She went back to the bedside drawers and searched for a nail file. She soon found one, and went back to the safe to begin jiggling it around in the lock.

Come on, come on, she whispered as she twisted and turned. Finally, the lock clicked and the door swung open.

The first thing she picked up was a passport. It was Nabyr's photo, but the name was Adil Rahman. Underneath was another passport, again with Nabyr's photo, but another new name. She memorized the names and moved onto the next document. It appeared to be a dossier on an individual: Matthew McGoldrick. Tsu immediately recognized the name. An American politician who she thought seemed schmoozy and superficial, but who everybody else appeared to adore.

The folder contained a range of details on McGoldrick, from his college background to his political campaigning.

What's the connection here? Tsu wondered. Was this 'the American' she had heard Osman referring to? *If he's working with Osman and Nabyr, he's a lot worse than schmoozy,* she thought. There was nothing else in the safe besides a few wads of various currencies, so she closed the door and started to think about the way out. The ledge was extremely unappealing.

She moved to the bedroom door and checked the lock. She only had to twist it to open the door. If somebody was outside in the corridor, she was in big trouble. But if she slipped off that ledge she was dead.

Trouble I can handle, she thought. *Death, not so much.*

She put her ear to the door to listen for any signs of activity on the other side. She could hear nothing but the faint droning beat of a song. She turned the key and pulled open the door. Her whole body relaxed as she saw the corridor was empty. She quietly closed the door behind her and headed down the corridor. As she neared the marble staircase, she decided that she had earned a glass of something strong.

"Are you lost?" a voice asked behind her. It was a voice she recognized. Nabyr.

She turned around to face him.

"How does someone get … in on the action around here?" she asked. After a painful pause, she saw Nabyr smile beneath his mask.

"Follow me," he said, taking her by the hand. He pulled her into the closest bedroom and shut the door. Then he pinned her up against the wall.

"Who are you?" he asked, his face an inch from hers.

"I'm with Osman," she told him.

"Good," Nabyr said. "He won't mind." He moved his hand up towards her face and touched her mask, trying to push it upwards.

"Wait," she said, putting her hand on his to stop him. "I want to keep it on."

"Well I want to see your face," he said, slapping her hand away. He grabbed her mask and began pulling.

She took hold of his wrist and held it firm, so he moved towards her mask with his other hand. She yanked his arm in a direction it was not supposed to go in, and he yelled in pain. She kept twisting until he was down on his knees.

"Okay! Okay!" he begged. "Please, let go. You can keep the mask on."

"It's too late now," she said. "You blew your chance." She let go of his wrist and bolted straight out of the door, leaving him inspecting his arm to see if it was broken.

Downstairs, she searched the living room for Osman. She found him in the corner of the room with his hands on a very tall, skinny woman.

"You need to take me home," she said.

"What? Why?"

"I'm sorry, I shouldn't have come. This isn't for me."

"Okay, but can't you just have a drink and relax?"

"Is this sort of thing even legal?" she asked. "This is an Islamic country."

"Let's not even talk about that," Osman said, suddenly active. "Don't talk about this party to anyone, do you understand?"

He took her by the hand and led her towards the door. When they got there, Nabyr was standing in the doorway.

"You said you like it rough," he said to Osman, "but she's next level ... "

24

DIVE BARS

With his untrimmed beard, fresh scars, and clothes donated by a French fisherman who was much smaller than him, it's fair to say Chris felt underdressed for the theater.

Nevertheless, the theater is where he now was. The only lead he had in Bordeaux was the name of an actress, Marianne Gigot, given to him by Ned via Jackie. An hour spent in an internet cafe had revealed little more than what he already knew—that she had barely survived a vicious attack that left her horribly injured.

There was some information online about her career before the attack, and nothing about any kind of career after it, which sadly wasn't surprising given that the attacker had left her disfigured.

The name of the attacker was given as Adham Mokrani, which Chris assumed was a pseudonym used by Basem Lellouche. Mokrani was still on the run, news reports said.

In the bar of the Le Dôme theater before the start of a performance, Chris knew he didn't have much time. He had no ticket for the show, and he knew everyone there that did would soon be drifting to their seats. He had a short window to chat to people who knew the local theater scene.

"I'm looking forward to this," he said in the best French he could manage to a woman dressed in a pearl necklace and a stunning gown. "The reviews have been fantastic."

The woman looked him up and down, then stared at his face with an expression that said she thought someone ought to call pest control.

Maybe she wasn't the best choice, Chris thought as she moved away. He looked around the room, his eyes landing on an elderly man whose last remaining wisps of hair were clinging onto his shining scalp for dear life. He was standing alone in a corner reading a program.

You'll do, Chris thought, making his way across the room.

"Excuse me, could you tell me where I can buy a program?" he asked the man, who then pointed past the tall marble pillars of the grand lobby to a stand at the opposite side.

"Thanks," Chris said. "I collect programs for everything that Yvette Romano is in."

"Yes, she is wonderful," the man replied.

"I think she may be my favorite. Possibly just behind Marianne Gigot," Chris added.

"Well, I don't think we'll be seeing her in anything more, sadly," the man replied.

"Yes, yes. Very sad. Did you hear what became of her after the attack?"

"I hear she turned to alcohol," the man told Chris. "She has been spotted being carried out of sleazy bars several times. Very sad."

Before Chris could get any further details, the bell rang and the old man moved quickly off to find his seat.

"Enjoy the show," he said to Chris as he walked away.

Thanks, but I'll be sleeping under a bridge by the time it's finished, Chris replied in his head.

SNOW WAS FALLING as Chris made his way past the palatial buildings surrounding Place de la Bourse, the city's famous square set along the Garonne river. He was heading for the Saint Marie district, for no other reason than it was well-known for having plenty of bars. If he couldn't find the area's seediest place and wait for a drunken actress to be escorted out, he could at least buy some cheap wine and keep warm for an hour or two.

He walked past bars with people huddled on rickety tables outside, refusing to give in to the cold, when he took another look over his shoulder to make sure he wasn't being followed. It was something he had gotten used to during his career, and had especially had to pay attention to during the last few weeks.

What he didn't like, was how many times he was seeing the guy in the black leather jacket. Around 100 meters behind, and having been on the same street at the same distance for a while.

I guess the wine will have to wait, Chris thought, knowing a surveillance detection route would have to come first. He needed to make three right turns, preferably down side streets where people were unlikely to follow randomly.

Down a narrow street with neon signs flashing 'girls' and 'shows', he saw the man loiter at the end of the street. He decided not to follow Chris, and instead ducked into a bar. But this had been the third turn, and the loitering had been too suspicious. So Chris stood and waited. He was sure the guy wouldn't be settling down to watch a girly show. He would be out again soon and trying to get back on Chris's tail.

Chris watched the doorway as the man duly emerged, his eyes darting in Chris's direction. Chris was half expecting him to turn and walk the opposite way, but the worse alternative happened. He turned Chris's way and began walking quickly towards him.

Chris was into fight mode immediately, making his way towards the man while keeping an eye on his hands for weapons. He produced none, but his hands were raised when Chris got to him. He used his long reach to knock the guy's arms aside as soon as he was close enough, then thrust a palm strike straight to his chin before the guy knew what was happening.

The man recovered from the blow and was trying to get his hands on Chris, but Chris was too quick, hammering in another blow to the head before twisting the man's arm behind his back and pinning him up against a wall.

"One more move and it's broken," Chris growled. Then he pulled a gun from under the man's belt and shoved the muzzle into the man's lower back.

"Why are you following me?" he asked.

"I'm trying to help you," the man said, breathing heavily.

"Sure you are. So why did you dart into a bar when I saw you were following me?"

"I knew you'd clocked me. I was trying to draw you into somewhere you were less likely to kill me."

"Who sent you?" Chris growled, pushing the man's arm further towards breaking.

"Ned."

The name took Chris by surprise. But he had no idea how the man knew it.

"How do I know you're telling the truth?" he asked.

"He said to ask you when you're going to invite him to share that expensive bottle of Glenlivet French Oak Reserve you've been hiding?"

Chris loosened his grip on the man, allowing him to turn around.

"How did you find me?" Chris asked.

"Ned knew you had a lead here—the actress. And he knew eventually you'd end up down around these dive bars."

"Well he was right, but I don't have much to go on. The last guy Ned sent to help me forgot to get half the details from him—his brain seems to have stopped working after years of too much booze. I hope you're more reliable."

"Well, I can't say I never touch a drop. But as far as I know, I still have all my faculties."

"Good. So where are we going?"

"Erm. I can't remember exactly. Just kidding. This way."

25

THE GOLDEN BOY

The singer's voice drifting through the bar was filled with a melancholy Chris had never heard before. The kind of sadness even great performers can't fake.

"*That's her,*" the man standing next to him said. Ned's contact had introduced himself as George, a Bordeaux native who knew the city inside out. He'd led Chris to a tiny bar down a cobbled alley in Saint Marie where he'd said they would find Marianne. He was right.

She finished her song, with a long, soft note, and left the stage without saying anything to the handful of people watching. She placed herself down at a round table close to the stage, and drank from a glass of clouded white pastis.

As Chris and George approached her table, she stared deep into Chris's eyes.

"Well, we don't find many people who look as good as

you drinking in here," she said in French while continuing to stare.

"Thanks," George replied. Chris was beginning to see why Ned liked this guy.

"Do you mind if we join you?" Chris asked.

"You, monsieur, can join me for as long as you like," the actress said.

"Your singing was beautiful," Chris told her.

"It was," George agreed."

"Thank you," Marianne said. "People don't want to look at me anymore, but some still like to listen to me."

Chris made a promise to himself to always look Marianne in the face, to avoid looking at her scars and always look her in the eyes.

"Do you live in Bordeaux?" she asked.

"Actually, I came to find you," Chris told her.

"Me? Whatever for?"

"Is there somewhere we could talk in private?"

"Intriguing," Marianne said. "I know just the place."

They finished their drinks, and she led them out of the bar and onto the street, walking over a growing layer of snow towards the river. After ten minutes, she showed them into a dark courtyard, then down a stairwell beside a wall covered in graffiti. She noticed as George shot Chris a look.

"Don't tell me you two big boys are scared of anything," Marianne said, smiling. She took out a key and unlocked a door at the bottom of the stairwell.

Inside, the room was completely dark, and it was the smell of dust that hit first. Marianne flicked the lights, and Chris could see they were in a cluttered dressing room, with racks of costumes lined up against red velvet walls.

"They forgot to take away my key," Marianne said as she turned on the bright lights around a large vanity mirror, staring at her face in the reflection.

"Can I get you guys a drink?" she asked, pulling a hip flask from her purse.

"Sure," George said.

"We'd like to talk to you about the man who attacked you," Chris told her, accepting a glass of whiskey. "I know it won't be easy for you to talk about, but it's important."

"Things that are easy to talk about usually aren't worth talking about," Marianne said, still looking at herself in the mirror.

"Thank you," Chris replied. "Do you know why he attacked you?"

"I was just in the wrong place. He was trying to kill my lover."

"And who was that?"

"Alain Brassant. He worked for the National Gendarmerie."

"Why did somebody want him dead?"

"He was a good police officer and a good man. And he was a rising star in the National Gendarmerie. Somebody didn't like that. Alain had been telling me somebody wanted him replaced. Someone with powerful connections. It wasn't really a surprise when they came for him."

"I didn't see his name in news reports," Chris said.

"Alain was a hero the night I was attacked. He was in another room when the attacker came into our bedroom. The bastard came for me first, and Alain burst in with a gun to defend me. That's what scared him off and saved my life. But after that, Alain broke down. He left the police force, and refused to ever talk about the incident again. Not to the press, not even to me."

Marianne paused, then added:

"Of course, I was the famous name, so the press focused on me."

She flung a silk scarf around her neck and pouted at herself in the mirror, as if she had suddenly forgotten the awful things she was talking about and had taken herself back to a different part of her past.

Chris briefly wondered if anyone could really be relied on. He wondered if everyone was either treacherous, insane, or permanently drunk. Knowing Marianne was his only chance of moving forward right now, he pushed the thoughts aside.

"These powerful connections," Chris said. "The people who wanted Alain out. Did he ever say who they were?"

"Not exactly," Marianne said. "He only said they were operating internationally, not just in France. It's a network, not a small group. They were trying to get their own people into positions of power."

"McGoldrick," Chris said.

"Who's that, dear?" Marianne asked.

"The golden boy of American politics."

"You think they're going to take him out?"

"No, I think he is one of them."

Marianne was pouting in the mirror again.

"I know you said he doesn't want to talk," Chris told her, "But do you know where we can find Alain?"

"Sure, dear. You can find him in Mountreuz Cemetery. He shot himself in the head last month."

Chris watched as Marianne drank deep from her glass of whiskey.

"I'm sorry to hear that," he said. "Thank you for talking to us."

"You're welcome, dear. But don't leave me alone until we finish this whiskey."

Chris glanced at the hip flask, wondering how much it could contain. Then he looked at Marianne's other hand, and the fresh bottle of whiskey she had pulled from a cupboard beneath the mirror.

CHRIS RUBBED warm water from his eyes and breathed deeply, not letting his hangover prevent him from enjoying a rare hot shower.

Once dressed in the perfectly fitting clothes George had given him, he walked through the safehouse apartment and into the living room. He made sure the curtains were closed, then he sat on the sofa and took out his new burner phone. George really had come through here. Well, actually, Ned had, Chris made sure to acknowledge.

The 'care package' had contained the phone, a Glock

19 pistol, a false passport, and money. It even contained a few other little goodies that might come in handy, like a tiny listening device and a compass. A few days earlier, he had nothing but the clothes on his back. And they were wet.

In the new phone were only two numbers. One was for a contact named 'The Man With The Plan.' In the name box for the other contact was simply: 'Call me first.'

Chris knew for a fact the first one would be Ned. He also knew the second would be his wife. He took a moment to make sure he was emotionally prepared, then called the second.

"Hello?" Alice answered after a few rings.

"Hey, it's me."

"Hey."

"How are you? Are you okay?"

"I'm okay."

Chris was quickly becoming concerned by his wife's terse replies.

"Can you talk? Is it safe?" He asked.

"Yeah. It's fine."

"I guess Ned got a phone to you. Pretty amazing, huh?"

"Yeah. It was just pushed through the mailbox one day, I don't even know who brought it."

"Well, it means we can talk."

"Yeah. Are you okay?" Alice asked.

"I am now. It's been a … challenging few weeks."

"Where are you now?"

"I probably shouldn't say."

"I understand."

"Alice, what's going on? You sound either afraid or sad. Which is it?"

"Well, I'm not afraid. Nobody came looking for me yet. As far as I know."

"So, what's wrong?"

Alice paused, then said:

"I know it's probably not a good time to tell you this, but in a way it will relieve you of a burden. I think it's over, Chris."

Chris waited, considering his response.

"You mean, we're over?"

"Yes."

"Without any warning?"

"It's not exactly out of the blue, is it? We haven't been right for years."

"But why now? You told me you believe I'm innocent."

"I do. But even if you are, how come it's you that ends up the victim of a conspiracy involving a high-level politician? You were doing boring admin work and you were supposed to be retiring."

"I'll explain everything one day, I promise."

"You'd have to explain twenty years of going out, doing your own thing, and leaving me in the dark."

"Look, we can talk when I get back. *If* I get back. Okay?"

"We can talk, but it won't change anything. Take care, Chris."

Chris looked at the phone, but Alice was gone.

As he sat in silence, thinking over every detail of the conversation they just had, there was a knock at the door.

He reached for his brand new gun, clicked off the safety, and approached the door.

"Don't tell me you've got that actress in there with you," he heard George's voice say. He unlocked the door and let him in.

"Were you followed?" Chris asked.

"No, of course not. I've done this a million and one times."

"Good ..."

Glass exploded into the room as the window shattered and bullets began hammering into the walls, relentless, ear-splitting noise filling the air as the two men crashed to the floor.

Breathing hard, Chris reached for his gun, then looked around to make sure George was okay. George was wide-eyed and staring back at Chris.

"How did the other million times end up?" Chris asked.

"I was *sure* I wasn't followed. Who the hell is it?"

"I don't know, but first we need to know *where* they are."

George took out his gun and very slowly began to bring his shoulders up to look towards the window, keeping his body behind the sofa he was using as a shield.

Chris watched him, ready to fire if George did. But all he saw was blood squirting from George's head, his neck snapping back before he slumped down.

Chris quickly dragged himself behind an overturned

table, making sure no part of him was exposed. He had his back to the window, but there was no way he could try to see what was going on.

He spotted a glass TV cabinet in front of him, and tried to see the window in its reflection.

From the balcony, a man dressed all in black jumped and landed deftly in the living room. In the reflection, Chris saw him coming closer, and knew he had to turn and fight.

26

CUTS LIKE A KNIFE

Tsu was getting sick of listening to this guy snore. But she was grateful that she didn't have to hear him doing worse than that. As she listened from afar, it sounded as if he returned to the hotel room every night alone. Clearly, paying for dinner at the swanky French restaurant was not enough to convince his dates to come back and take part in the kinds of things he liked to take part in.

Listening to hours of snoring was a means to an end. When he was awake, Osman was occasionally making and taking phone calls about things that Tsu was very interested in. So far, she had managed to ascertain that an event was being planned in which a group of people would be trapped and murdered, and that an 'American' was somehow involved in the planning. If the American was McGoldrick, then Nabyr was involved too.

During the three days since the party, the only thing she had done other than listen was to inform her superior that he should let the Americans know their possible presidential candidate, McGoldrick, was someone they should be keeping a very close eye on.

After three days of listening, she was rewarded for her patience.

"He has finally arranged to meet us," Osman told somebody on the phone. "In the desert south of Sanankoroba."

He listened to the other person's reply, and then said:

"No, it's better if we go in one car. There's less chance of being followed." A pause. "Well, if you think I'm paranoid, he certainly is. He has just resurfaced after the Pakati Stadium attack. Meet me at the agreed place, 7pm tomorrow."

Tsu knew exactly what the Pakati Stadium attack was. It was the work of SIA group. Tsu believed, and in truth feared, that the person Osman was about to meet was Sheikh Habib — the group's leader. A man absolutely devoid of mercy and willing to do anything for his cause, no matter how brutal.

She realized tomorrow would likely involve a period of monotonous waiting followed by high levels of anxiety and possibly a risk to her life. A strange combination, but one she was used to.

THE NEXT MORNING, she was back at the barbecue restaurant across the street from the hotel, her scooter waiting and ready to go around the corner. She knew Osman's meeting wasn't until the evening, but she couldn't let him out of her sight all day, just in case. She sat sipping black coffee, trying to master the art of drinking it while wearing the niqab she hoped would obscure her from Osman.

The afternoon sun was casting long shadows across the street when Osman finally emerged from the hotel. Tsu kept her eye on him as she left the restaurant and moved towards her scooter. She could see he was leaving the hotel on foot.

Luckily, the traffic was so packed that it was moving at the same pace as pedestrians. She edged through the city as Osman picked his way between cars, scooters, and sheets that were laid out on the street with goods for sale, the vendors sitting on the road beside them.

She realized he was likely heading to Banjara Market, the meeting point he had mentioned the day before. She knew that crowded markets are good places to remain obscured.

When Osman eventually made it there, he spent the next hour browsing the cluttered stalls, looking like any other punter. But occasional turns of his head made it clear he was checking for any tails. Tsu, meanwhile, had to browse like she was any other punter too, mixing among people at the packed market that was getting even more crowded now the sun had set.

At exactly 7pm, she saw Osman turn to look at a battered white pickup truck, then casually walk towards it. Through the window, she thought she could see Nabyr sitting in the truck, but she didn't have time to stare. She was back to her scooter, getting the engine running and moving onto the street fifty meters behind the truck.

Getting out of the city was slow going, but she knew that once they did, being discreet would be more difficult. Within an hour, they had left the edge of southern Bamako and were into a desert of red sand covered with small, hardy shrubs.

Tsu was falling as far behind as she could. She turned her lights off to stay as hidden as possible, but that brought its own danger. The road was rough and full of potholes, and she couldn't see them until they were buffeting her tires, throwing her from side to side, and sometimes almost off the bike.

After thirty minutes of trying to stay on the bike while keeping an eye on the vehicle way ahead, they passed through the small town of Sanankoroba and emerged back into the desert on the other side. This was the area Osman had said the meeting was taking place, and Tsu was hoping to see the truck slow down and stop somewhere soon.

It was hard to tell through the dust and darkness, but she thought she saw the truck move off the road. When she reached the same point, she could see a tiny farmhouse, the truck parked up outside.

She continued a short distance, then slowly brought her scooter to a stop. She laid it down in the desert dirt to keep it out of sight, and made her way cautiously on foot towards the farmhouse.

Only a small light, maybe a lamp or a few candles, was coming from the farmhouse window. It looked like most of the windows had no glass, which would make listening easier.

She stepped gently across the hard ground, looking around to make sure nobody was outside the building. She was beginning to hear the sound of voices as she made her way around the darkest side of the house, walking in a crouch before finally getting on the ground and leopard crawling beside the wall.

Under a window where voices seemed to be emanating the loudest, she stopped. She could hear a voice speaking in Arabic, and then somebody translating into English.

"He's saying the transportation will cost extra," the translator said, and she realized the voice was Osman's.

"No. No. That was not the fucking deal," someone replied, and Tsu was almost certain it was Nabyr. "The payment includes the weapons and the transportation. And he knows that. Tell him to stop playing games with us."

After a few more translated sentences, Nabyr said:

"We're already paying him to take the risk of transportation. What does he think the money is for? Tell him to have the weapons, with specifications exactly as agreed, in Rabat by December 10th. Those terms or we walk away now."

A short time later, Nabyr said to Osman:

"Good. Give him the money. Half now, half later. And let's get out of this shithole."

It sounded like the discussion was coming to an end, and Tsu wasn't sure she wanted to take the risk of hanging around on the off chance there were any more details.

She had made the decision to move away from the farmhouse when a knee thudded sharply into her back, knocking the wind out of her. Her head was yanked back by the hair, and she felt the terrifying edge of a knife blade on her neck.

THEN THE BULLETS

L ying on his back on the carpeted floor, Chris knew he had only a few seconds to make a decision. If he put his head above the overturned table that was hiding him, the other man in the room could get a shot at him.

Looking up, he could see there was a glass light fitting in the center of the ceiling. He aimed and shot at it only once, sending glass shattering around the room. Immediately he turned, aiming over the table while the man was briefly distracted. He fired two quick shots, but without time to aim properly they landed in the man's left shoulder.

Chris ducked behind the table again as the man fired back before slumping to the ground. Chris knew that the guy would be injured, but still capable of shooting. There was a moment of silence, and Chris wondered if he had got closer to the man's chest than he thought.

Then the bullets came, hard and fast, tearing through

the wood. Chris could hear the table quickly breaking up around him. Out of options, he stood and fired in the direction the bullets were coming from. But the man was gone, a pool of blood in his place.

Chris stepped from behind the table, the noise of gunshots still in his ears even though the room was now quiet. He knew he was out of bullets, and he could only hope the other guy was too.

As he trod carefully across the carpet towards the pool of blood, his head was rocked to the left by a savage blow. He stumbled but stayed on his feet, turning as the man tried to land another.

The chunky metal rail the man was swinging almost snapped Chris's arm as he defended himself. The blows kept on coming, but through instinct and desperation Chris managed to land a kick on the man's knee, making him yell out in pain.

The guy dropped his blunt weapon and went for Chris's throat. It was now a simple battle of strength. Chris blocked him and stopped him from getting his hands on his throat, so the man swung his left fist hard into Chris's jaw.

Chris got his hands up and blocked a second shot. Now in a wrestle, Chris knew he had to get the guy against a wall. Gritting his teeth, he tried to maneuver the man a few feet. He was a strong guy, but Chris slowly moved him towards the wall. It was the chance he needed.

He swung his right forearm and connected with the

man's trachea, right where he wanted it. Shocked by the strike to his windpipe, the man froze.

Chris landed blow after blow on the man's head, throwing elbows and punches. Finally, the guy slumped to the ground. Chris looked around for something to use and saw the metal rail that had previously been used on him.

He pushed it against the guy's throat. The man's eyes were half open and looking at Chris. But he was unable to defend himself, and Chris pushed down hard, squeezing and squeezing. Finally, all life was gone from his body.

Chris took a moment to compose himself and catch his breath, but he knew he had to get out. First, he had to search the man he had killed. The only things on him were his empty gun, a few notes, and a small key. There was no ID. Chris took the notes and the key, then got moving.

He could hear the sound of sirens as he searched for a way out. The building's main entrance was now a no-go. He looked down the corridor and saw a fire escape at the back of the building.

He pushed down the bar and went out onto the narrow staircase. He could soon see the fire escape route would lead him out onto the main street. He had to look for an alternative.

He saw that if he jumped from the staircase, he could land in a small enclosure meant for trash. But the trash wasn't the problem ... the drop was. He guessed it must have been ten feet. But there was no choice.

Without thinking any further, he leapt over the black bars of the fire escape and fell. Previous training had taught him how to fall properly, but the impact still sent a shock through his whole body. He didn't have time to check if anything was broken.

He opened the gate of the trash area and stepped into a narrow alley covered in snow. He picked up some of the snow and used it to wash the blood from his face. Then, moving away from the sound of the sirens, he walked calmly through the narrowest streets he could find.

As he walked, he reached into his pocket. Attached to the small key was a fob with a three-digit number and the words 'Gare de Lyon-Part-Dieu.' Guessing it must be a key for a locker at Lyon railway station, Chris decided where he was going next. He had to get some place well away from Bordeaux, and Lyon had just become his destination.

28

A TRICKY SITUATION

The frost-hardened fields and sleepy towns of rural France passed Chris's eyes but barely registered in his consciousness as the train rolled towards Lyon.

He was too busy trying to discreetly observe everyone on the train, watching for somebody watching him. He now knew he was on the run from both law enforcement and an extensive network of dangerous people who had him, and apparently many others, in their sights.

The sky was a bruised gray when the train pulled into Lyon's run-down railway station, and Chris was making a mental note of the faces around him. If he saw any of them again after he left the station, that would be cause for serious concern.

He also needed privacy before he even left the station because he wanted to get a look in the locker. He stepped off the train onto the crowded platform, picking his way through the shuffling crowd. He found a sign stating that lockers were on the second floor, and made his way up.

After a discreet glance around to make sure nobody was following him, he found the right locker and pulled the key from his pocket. He pushed it into the lock and turned, anxious about what he would find.

Inside was only one item. A photo of a man with white, wavy hair. The name was written beneath the photo, but Chris knew who it was already. Walter Schneider.

Schneider was a Swiss politician who had been in the news in recent months for pushing a particular cause. He wanted to extend the powers of international governments to freeze the assets of groups and individuals suspected of criminal activity. It was a risky cause to pursue, and Chris admired Schneider for doing it.

He made another visual sweep of the area to check that he wasn't being watched, then made his way out of the station. He now knew Schneider was a target of the same people who had tried to kill him, and he knew it was likely the attack would be soon. The question was: where?

At the station exit he found a map of the area, and saw that Bibliothèque municipale de Lyon was very nearby. He hoped he could get internet access at the public library, and headed towards it.

Inside the large, utilitarian building, he found what he was looking for. He logged on and typed in 'Walter Schneider."

'Schneider to speak at UN Congress on Crime Prevention,' read one of the headlines. Chris clicked through news articles and saw that the congress was being held in three days' time at Palais des Nations, home of the United Nations Office in Geneva.

It had to be there, Chris thought. Whoever wanted him dead obviously thought the symbolism of assassinating him at a crime prevention conference sent the kind of sick message they wanted.

A decision was made quickly. Ned's care package had contained a wad of 200 euro notes, and now was the time for Chris to start spending it. Traveling by car would free him from anymore stares from train passengers, and from wondering if they were staring because of his disheveled look or because they had seen his face on TV.

He hoped his new scruffy look made him appear as differently as possible from how he usually looked: clean-cut and well-dressed, according to the many people who for some reason had to frequently comment on his smart appearance.

But that appearance was long gone, and he took his new unkempt self out of the library and onto a tram heading towards the city's eastern suburbs. He decided he would stay on the tram until he saw one of two things: an area with used car dealerships, or a run-down area where people might be persuaded to part with cars quickly for cash.

The tram terminated in the Albi district, where brown tower blocks were packed together, graffiti decorating the walls at their base and laundry flying high in the sky from windows all the way up to their top floors.

The rain was falling hard as Chris walked the dirty

streets, past boarded-up stores and homes with broken windows. He knew there would be no dealerships here, but even a small repair shop would do. After more than two hours of walking and staring down occasional hostile glances from the few people he passed on the street, he noticed a sign saying 'car wash.'

He approached and saw a few cars on the forecourt. A couple of them had cardboard signs with prices on the windshields. There also seemed to be a few repairs going on in the back.

He strode onto the property and could hear voices coming from the far side, so he walked towards them. There were three men standing around a car, one of them in overalls and the other two in oil-stained jeans and T-shirts.

"I want to buy a car," Chris announced immediately. "I need it today—and no paperwork."

The three men stared at him in silence. They seemed to be weighing up why he had suddenly turned up in their area speaking French in an accent that was nowhere near local.

"Which one do you want?" one of the man asked finally.

"I'll need a quick look at them," Chris said.

"No paperwork means you pay cash."

He knew this was a tricky situation, because offering hundreds of euros in cash for a car would obviously let them know he had a wad of cash on him.

"Of course," he said, confirming what everyone already knew.

The men were staring again.

Chris gestured towards the forecourt, suggesting they go take a look at the cars. But there were only stares and silence. He sensed the atmosphere was changing. He could see the biggest man going for a wrench, a look of grim determination on his face.

Chris pulled his gun from his belt. He knew it was empty from the firefight in the apartment, but they didn't. He pointed it straight at the big guy's head.

"How about a different arrangement?" he said. "You give me the best car on the forecourt, and I'll let you keep your brain inside your tiny skull?"

The men froze.

It quickly became obvious that even if these guys could bully locals out of a bit of money, they weren't used to having guns pointed at them. All three men put their hands up in front of their chests, and Chris took them out onto the forecourt.

Twenty minutes later, he had inspected a Citroën ZX as best he could and was being handed the keys. He got in the car and started the engine, which roared smoothly to life.

Well, it's in better shape than the boat, he thought as he accelerated, forcing the big guy to jump out of the way as he pulled off the forecourt.

29

THE GREEN-EYED MAN

Slowly opening her eyes, Tsu saw her head was resting on a filthy concrete floor. Then she saw the blood. It was dark, dry blood in a patch that extended from her head out almost a meter.

That's when she noticed the pain, and she knew the blood was hers. She lifted herself up and put her hand to where the pain was worst. She looked at her fingers and saw only a little dried blood. The wound was obviously not fresh, and she knew it wouldn't have been treated.

She tried to stand, but something stopped her. Her other hand wouldn't move. She turned to look at it and saw she was chained to a wall. She checked her feet and saw they were bound together.

She quickly pieced together the situation she was in. She remembered somebody catching her as she listened to the conversation at the farmhouse. Whether she was still at the farmhouse or elsewhere she had no idea, but wherever it was she knew there were few worse places in the world to be.

Looking around the room, she could see she would be lacking even the most basic comforts. There was no mattress, no window, only a bright and flickering light on the ceiling. The only thing other than concrete was a bowl of dirty water.

Worst of all, there were patches of dried blood in various parts of the room, suggesting she was not the first person to receive this kind of hospitality.

The room was dilapidated, with small holes in the walls. It looked as if it had been attacked with bullets at some point, possibly even bombs.

She stretched herself out as far as she could to see if she could reach the water. It was almost out of reach, but she stretched herself as far as she could manage, straining every muscle. Her whole body felt in pain, and she knew her head wasn't the only injury.

She managed to get her fingertips onto the edge of the bowl and tried to drag it towards her. It came slowly, and some of the water splashed out as the bowl scraped across the floor.

When she could inspect the water more closely, she could see how dirty it really was. It was dark brown. Insects were floating in it; some dead and some alive. She was desperately thirsty, but she knew that drinking that water could be worse than thirst. Dysentery would just worsen the dehydration … and possibly kill her.

"Hey!" she tried to scream, but her voice was weak. She cleared her throat and tried again.

"Hey!"

When nobody came, she shuffled towards the metal door and found she was close enough to kick it with both her bound feet.

She booted the door several times as hard as she could, the noise echoing around the room. As she was kicking, she finally heard the door being opened.

A man in long, brown robes entered the room, his head and face mostly obscured by a black turban. All Tsu could see were brown eyes. He said nothing, he just bent down and slapped Tsu hard across the cheek.

"Water!" she begged, ignoring the slap.

He looked at the bowl of brown water and gestured towards it. She shook her head. He picked up the bowl, and looked right into Tsu's eyes while he slowly poured it all onto the floor. He then left the room, slamming the door hard behind him.

Tsu didn't know how long she was alone in the room after that, but she estimated it must have been at least a further twenty-four hours without water. The room was oppressively hot, and she was beginning to feel the serious effects of dehydration.

As she was mulling over what the consequences of trying to get attention might be, she heard the lock in the door being turned. It opened and the same man walked in, holding a bowl of water.

He crouched down beside Tsu and showed her a bowl of clean water.

"Thank you," she said, looking into his eyes.

He stood, took a step back, and poured the water

onto the floor again. Tsu was devastated as she saw the clean water going to waste. It was too far away even to lick it up from the filthy floor. Without a word, the man turned and left.

She was filled with rage, but she knew that being angry would waste too much energy. She made herself calm down as quickly as possible, then she lay down and closed her eyes.

Through hours of unconsciousness, fitful waking, and vivid dreams about lush desert cities, she went without water. Pain was trying to wake her, but she didn't want to be awake.

Until a loud noise gave her no choice.

She could hear the angry voices of two men shouting at each other.

"You stupid idiot!" one of them said, in French. "We need her alive!"

"She is alive!" the other voice replied.

"When did you check?"

"I don't know. Recently. She's fine! She looks tough."

The shouting stopped, then the door burst open. A shorter man in similar robes entered the room, carrying a plastic bottle filled with water. He knelt down beside Tsu, and she could see his eyes were a fierce green.

He held the bottle to her lips ... and she drank. She wanted to drink the whole lot, but he pulled the bottle away.

"Slowly," he said, putting it back to her lips. When she had finally finished drinking, she thanked him and asked for food.

"Okay," the man said.

A minute later, he returned with bread. It was stale, but it was one of the best things Tsu had ever tasted. Feeling as if life had re-entered her body, she lay down again and slept.

When she awoke, it was because somebody was lifting her up. She saw it was the man with the green eyes. He pulled a key from his belt and unlocked the cuffs that held her to the wall. Then, with her feet still bound, he put his hands under shoulders and carried her out of the room.

Tsu was hoping for another moment of compassion from this man. She was taken to a completely dark room and was sat down in a chair. By the time she realized there had been no compassion at all, it was too late. She felt her hands being chained to a table in front of her, and the lights went on.

She saw the green-eyed man standing in front of her, and knew the food and water had only been given so that she could be kept alive long enough to be interrogated. The man rolled up his sleeves before opening a case that contained work tools. He pulled out a hammer and pliers, then turned to face Tsu with a look of pure evil in his eyes.

30

HAMMER TO FALL

"Who do you work for?" the green-eyed man asked. It was the tenth time he had asked the question.

"I work alone."

"With what purpose?"

"I told you, I won't answer any more questions."

She looked into the man's eyes. She couldn't see much of his face, but she was trying to get a sense of his character. She knew that not everyone who is given the task of torture has the stomach to carry it out. She also knew that terrorists could be either fanatics or simply people who allow themselves to be recruited in return for payment.

"I've been through all of this before," she told the man. "It's only pain. A better move is to give me what I want. Then I'll give you what you want."

The man looked angry about being dictated to, but hesitated.

"What do you want?" he asked.

"Clean water, food, and something to sleep on. That's all. Then, tomorrow, I'll tell you what you want to know."

"Why should I believe you?"

"I have no loyalty to the person who paid me. I don't care who knows about them."

"What's your name?" the man asked.

"Tomorrow."

"No! Now!" he demanded.

"I'll tell you everything tomorrow."

"I decide when! Not you!"

He turned to the tool box and pulled out a hammer. He walked back towards Tsu, his face full of rage. He raised the hammer high over his head, positioning it above her right hand.

"Name!" he demanded.

"Please," she replied. "If I hate you, I can't talk to you. No matter what you do." She still had no idea if he would really hurt her or not. Maybe he had no idea either. Then, the hammer came down.

Tsu lifted the whole table off the ground, her hands still cuffed to it. It was heavy but she could lift it, and she heaved it to one side.

While the man tried to figure out what was going on, she lifted it as high as she could, then whipped it through the air. The sharp corner connected with the man's chest, and he screamed in pain.

She used all her remaining strength to lift the table even higher and swung it again. This time it smashed into his jaw, knocking him to the ground.

As she tried to keep herself away from him, there were footsteps outside the room. The brown-eyed man came crashing in. He saw what was happening and grabbed Tsu by the shoulders, dragging her back into the chair and pinning her down.

The green-eyed man was frozen still.

"What the hell?" Brown-Eyes yelled at him. He pulled himself together and helped to pin her down.

"Cell!" Brown-Eyes said. "Cell!" Then he took out a key and unlocked Tsu's hands from the table.

The two men dragged her out of the room and back towards her cell. They flung her in, locking the door as she fell to the floor. She could hear them arguing as they walked away.

As the next hours passed, they brought no food or clean water. All she had was another bowl of disgusting water that looked like it had been pissed in. She wasn't even sure if they meant it for her to drink or to go to the toilet in. But if they didn't bring new water soon, she knew she would have to drink it.

She could hear the two men's voices coming from somewhere in the building. She thought they must be making new plans for her. But she was making a plan of her own.

In the cracked walls of the room, she had noticed parts of metal frames were exposed. They were rusting badly, and given enough force they might break. This time, the men hadn't cuffed one of her hands to the wall, but they had cuffed both together. It made moving around easier even if it meant she had no hand completely free.

First, she found a weak-looking part of the wall and chipped away at the plaster, scraping and hammering at it with the metal of her cuffs. When a good sized piece of metal was finally exposed, she began working away at that.

The cuffs were becoming rougher and sharper, which made the task easier the longer she did it. She wanted a piece of metal around a foot long, and worked at sawing a cut in either end.

In the awful heat and with no water, it was exhausting work. But she didn't know how much longer they would let her live … or what they would do with her if she was alive.

After several hours, she hoped the piece of metal was loose enough to pull out. With a few tugs, it came out of the wall and was in her hands. First, she used it to cut the plastic tie on her legs. Then, she started the noise.

She began howling as if in the most awful agony. While she wailed, she kept an eye on the door. It flew open.

"Quiet!" Green-Eyes yelled as he walked towards her. His hand was open, ready to slap her. When he was within distance, Tsu thrust the jagged piece of metal deep into his stomach. He didn't scream, he just gulped as the air disappeared from his body.

She pulled him down onto the floor next to her, where he was a perfect height to land a crushing headbutt right on the bridge of his nose. His head bounced off the ground, then his eyes rolled back in his head.

She desperately fumbled around his belt and pockets, looking for the key to her cuffs. She could hear footsteps coming towards the room as she searched. She found a small key and tried to put it in the lock on the cuffs, her hands slipping with sweat. She rattled the key around but it wouldn't fit in the lock.

Brown-Eyes entered the room. Her hands weren't free, but she was now on her feet. She noticed for the first time how much taller she was than him. He stood frozen for a moment, staring at her. Then, he moved towards her. But she was faster.

She stepped close to him and swung her hands, cuffed together in a double fist. She connected with his head and he stumbled, so she swung again. He hit the ground.

She went to kick him in the balls, drawing her foot back as far as it would go for maximum impact. But a searing pain pierced into her standing leg. She looked down and saw the man had bitten her, his teeth now covered in her blood.

Stepping away, she tried to ignore the pain and get back on the attack. But he was getting to his feet. He flew at her, knocking her off balance and stumbling back towards the wall. She put her hands up to defend herself but the man was on her, his eyes now inches from hers.

He gritted his teeth and growled as he tried to get his hands on her throat. She forced him away with her arms, and in frustration he swung wildly and connected with her chin.

She cried out in pain but didn't stop moving. She managed to make enough room to release a kick and landed on his knee cap, snapping his leg. He wailed over the sound of snapping bone.

Tsu took her chance and maneuvered herself behind him. She moved the cuffs over his head and then yanked back, the chain digging into his throat. She pulled and pulled, her energy slipping away.

He struggled hard, and she didn't know if she would have enough strength left to choke him. He began to weaken, but Tsu was exhausted. He had stopped moving and his eyes were closed, but she could still hear weak, slow breathing. She realized she didn't need to pull any longer. Pushing would be easier.

She let the man fall to the ground, then dragged the bowl of water towards him. Lifting up his head by the hair, she put the bowl under him and shoved his face into the water. Resting all of her weight on top of him, she let him drown in the filthy water that was meant for her.

31

SHIMMERING DESERT HEAT

Tsu stepped over to the green-eyed man she had rendered unconscious. She took her time to search him and find the right key for her cuffs. She found the key and freed herself, then dragged him out of her cell, down a dimly lit corridor, and into the room he had recently taken her for interrogation.

After handcuffing him to the table, she slapped him hard across the face. He didn't wake up. She walked back into the corridor and headed for the room she had previously heard the men's voices coming from.

She found a sparsely furnished room with a sofa, a radio, and a tiny kitchen. She turned on the tap, took a long drink, then picked up a large bowl and filled it with water. Collecting a towel on her way out, she headed back to the interrogation room.

She tipped the man's head back and placed the towel over his face. Then, she poured water onto the towel.

Green-Eyes immediately came coughing and

spluttering back to consciousness. Tsu removed the cloth and loomed over him

"What's the plan for Rabat?" she asked.

The man's eyes darted around the room as he tried to figure out where he was. She placed the towel over his face and tipped more water. She knew from grim experience how awful the sensation of drowning was. Finally, she stopped and removed the towel.

"What's the plan for Rabat?"

"I don't know! We just take weapons. They don't tell plan."

From above, Tsu stared hard into the man's eyes. She sensed he was telling the truth.

"Where are you delivering the weapons?"

"I don't know."

She placed the towel over his face again.

"Okay! Okay!" he said, his voice muffled under the wet towel.

"Deliver near Mechra Lake east of Rabat. An old tile factory where the river flows north."

"Is the date still December 10th?"

"Yes, I think."

"What else do you know?"

"Nothing."

"What kind of weapons?"

"I think guns, but I don't know."

Tsu only had to lift the towel a little closer to his face.

"My job is guard you!" he cried. I don't know all details. I don't bring weapons."

"Anything else you want to tell me before this goes back on your face?"

"They said to tell our guys in Europe that if we have opportunity to kill a CIA guy, we should kill."

"Which CIA guy?"

"Name Collins. I don't know much. Just if we find out where he is, kill him."

One more look into the man's eyes told Tsu he had told her everything he knew. Without another word, she walked over to the tool box. She took out a screwdriver from the box, and walked back to stand behind the man.

Swinging from high above her head, she brought the screwdriver down and plunged it into his heart. He gasped, shuddered, then fell forward dead.

I wouldn't be so cruel as to let you sit there for days and die of thirst, Tsu thought. *Even though you would.*

She walked to the kitchen, filled up a plastic bottle with water, and ate the small amount of food she could find. She winced as she used some soap to clean her wounds, then made her way cautiously out of the building.

All around her was desert. For miles in every direction, red dirt covered with nothing but brown shrubs. The only thing on the horizon was shimmering heat. Looking up to check the position of the sun, she picked a direction, and began to walk.

32

HOPE ON THE HORIZON

For hours, Tsu walked under the fierce sun. She kept a sure and steady pace, immediately dismissing any thoughts that the desert might get the better of her.

But she had barely eaten or slept for so long that her body wasn't at its usual strength. When she began to feel dizzy, she walked harder, determined to win the mental and physical battle. When she tried and occasionally stumbled, she cursed herself for her weakness.

Night was falling when the desert air filled with the sound of animals, howling and crying as they emerged after the hottest part of the day.

Keeping the same direction was now very difficult. She thought about simply lying down on the desert floor and resting until morning, but she told herself she had to keep going.

Then, something gave her hope. A slowly moving light on the horizon. The way it moved, it looked like it belonged to a vehicle. Twenty minutes later, she saw the same thing again.

The sight gave her a massive boost, and she pushed on as fast as she could walk. By the time she saw a third vehicle, she could just about make out the sound of its engine.

Knowing that traffic would grow less as the night got later, she began running, tripping over bumps but staying on her feet. Finally, she was standing at the side of the road. Now, she had to make somebody stop. After ten minutes, a car approached and she stuck out her thumb, but it flew by without the driver even acknowledging her.

The next time, she wasn't taking any chances. A vehicle's lights emerged from the darkness and she saw it was a large SUV. She stepped into the road directly in front of it, pushing both hands outwards.

She saw the driver's face as he realized there was something in the road. He slammed on the brakes, making the car swerve from side to side. It screeched to a halt in a diagonal position across both lanes a few meters in front of her.

Before the driver could move off, she ran over and hammered on the window. A terrified family stared back at her.

"Help!" she shouted in French, making sure she looked distressed. After what she had been through, it came easily.

Expressions softened when the people in the car saw it was a woman. A back door opened, and she immediately climbed in. As she sat, she could hear the driver scolding somebody for opening the door, and she turned to see a girl of maybe seven or eight years old sitting next to her, smiling.

"Thank you!" she said, smiling back.

The driver was not so friendly. His face was a mixture of anger and confusion.

"I was lost in the desert," Tsu explained. "You saved my life. Thank you."

Wordlessly, the driver straightened the vehicle and started down the road. A man and a woman were in the front seats, and finally the woman spoke.

"Are you okay?" she asked.

"If you have food or water, I would be so grateful."

A rustling sound made her turn towards the girl, who was holding out a huge bag of potato chips. Tsu smiled as she took a handful.

While they were happily sharing the chips, the man asked gruffly:

"Where do you want to go?"

"That depends where I am."

"What?"

"Where am I? I don't know where I am."

"Adrar."

"Where is that?"

"You don't know what country?"

"No!"

"Algeria. The middle."

"Algeria. Wow. I need to get to Morocco. Can you help me?"

"No."

The two females in the car shouted at the man for being rude.

"The border is closed," the man said.

"I'll worry about that later," Tsu told him. Crossing borders at official points wasn't her general M.O. in any case.

Then, the woman spoke:

"My brother will take you to the border. He has nothing to do."

"Thank you so much. I'm sorry, but I don't have any money."

"Well then, you'd better have some good stories to keep him entertained."

It was almost light by the time they reached the desert city of Ghardaia, pulling up outside a whitewashed home where a large, beaming man was standing next to a truck and waving. An earlier phone call meant that the brother was reading and waiting.

"My brother, Farid," the woman said. "He is ready."

Tsu stepped out of the car and walked towards Farid.

"Oh, my!" Farid announced as she approached. "I swear I have never seen anybody so…"

Tsu sometimes got a little annoyed by people telling her she was beautiful, because she found it difficult to know how to respond. But she was prepared to be friendly to this guy who was helping her.

"…tired. I think you are the most tired person I have ever seen!"

Tsu laughed while silently admonishing herself for being vain and presumptuous.

"Please," Farid said, opening the car door to reveal a huge back seat. "Sleep."

Tsu thanked Farid's family for everything, then climbed into the car. Despite feeling guilty and being jostled by the bumps in the road, she slept the full ten-hour journey to the border.

When she awoke, Farid was switching off the engine and climbing out of the vehicle. Bleary eyed, Tsu stepped out to join him. They were surrounded by the majesty of the Sahara Desert on all sides, now without even shrubs to cover the sand. Only the border fence, 200 meters away, the soft contours of dunes, and the distant Atlas Mountains over the border punctuated the landscape.

"I'm sorry I didn't entertain you on the journey," Tsu said.

"That's okay," Farid replied. "You kept me entertained by talking in your sleep, telling me all your secrets."

Fear flashed quickly across Tsu's face.

"Joking!" Farid told her. "Only snoring, no problem."

He reached into the trunk and pulled out a small backpack.

"You will need all of this," he said. He opened the bag to show Tsu what was inside, and pulled out a flask. "Tea! Very delicious tea."

Next was something wrapped in brown paper, which he peeled back.

"Homemade cake, made by my wife. And honey, made in our village. So wonderful."

"Wow," Tsu said. "Thank you."

Farid reached into the bag again, pulling something else out.

"And this."

Tsu raised her eyebrows in amazement as Farid held out a beautiful dagger in front of her.

"I'm guessing that's not for the cake?" Tsu asked.

"No!" Farid laughed. "You will need to cut the fence." He handed her the backpack and the dagger. He pulled a few crumpled ten-dollar bills from his pocket and handed her those too.

"Left over from a business trip some years ago. They will be accepted anywhere," he told her. Then he pointed south along the fence. "Walk ten miles that way. It's usually not guarded in that area, but be careful. On the other side, head for the mountains."

After thanking Farid profusely which seemed to confuse him, she walked into the desert while his vehicle roared away.

Feeling so much stronger than the last time she was walking through the desert, she covered the ten miles in no time. She was desperate to get across and make it to Rabat, but she knew that the right thing to do was to wait until nightfall. It was late afternoon, and the sun was already beginning to set.

As the sun fell, Tsu stared out at the desert as the sand turned an enchanting pink color, and she was briefly at peace. But it was time to move. She headed towards the fence, feeling like she was the only person for a hundred miles. She was keeping an eye out for life nonetheless.

She knelt at the base of the fence and took out the dagger, momentarily pausing to admire its beauty in the moonlight. Then, she used it to slice through the wire with incredible ease. She had soon made a big enough hole to be able to get onto her belly in the sand and roll through.

After straightening the mesh of the fence as best she could, she was on the move. She wanted to run, but she knew she had to conserve energy. She strode quickly on, only the sound of her breathing filling the desert night.

Then, an explosion of noise. A barking dog, so close to her and so loud, but she couldn't tell which direction it was. The impact hit her hard from the right, and she fell under the weight of the huge dog. It was quickly on top of her, trying to get its jaws to her throat.

She pulled her knees up in front of her to protect her vital organs, and raised her left arm in front of her face. The dog bit it repeatedly. It was ripping her arm to shreds, but she knew if she moved it she would be dead.

Her right hand was fumbling around desperately for the dagger, but she couldn't lay her hand on it.

The dog was putting all of its weight on her arm, pushing it down and moving closer to her face, it's bloodthirsty growl so close to her ear.

Suddenly, she felt the ornate handle of the dagger in her hand, but she couldn't pull it out from under her. Grimacing as she strained to move herself, she rolled left just enough to be able to release the dagger, and pulled it out from under her.

She swung it straight and true towards the dog's neck, landing bang in the middle of its throat.

The growling turned briefly to yelping, but as she dragged the knife through flesh, the noise faded away. She pushed the dog off of her, its lifeless body rolling onto the desert floor.

Tsu lay on her back staring up at the cloudless night sky, breathing hard. She didn't even want to look at her left arm, but she knew she had to.

It was a terrible mess, but the dog hadn't been able to get enough of a grip to take any big chunks. She looked at the dead animal beside her, and saw it looked wild. She had feared it belonged to border patrol, so that, at least, was a relief.

She looked around for her bag and saw it had been flung a few meters during the attack. After slowly bringing herself to her feet and walking over to pick up the bag, she took out the honey.

She opened the jar and poured the thick substance onto her injured arm. She gritted her teeth as she rubbed it in, knowing that its natural antibacterial properties would be good for her wounds.

Using her good hand, she ripped a piece of fabric from her shirt and used it to bandage up the wounds. Then, she walked, heading northwest towards where the ridge of the mountains was lit by moonlight. Injured and now terrified of wild animals, she walked on through the desert for another six hours.

Finally, as the first light of dawn touched the edges of dunes, she reached the town of Mhamid. The small town had long been a final outpost of civilization where trade caravans converged before heading out into the dessert. It had a bus station, and with only one road through the town it didn't take long to find.

With very few people around at the early hour, Tsu was happy there was nobody to overhear the phone call she was about to make. She picked up one of the pay phones and made a collect call to the United States. Specifically, to an office in Langley, Virginia. She then heard it diverting to a cell phone.

"Ned Henry," a voice said when the call was finally answered.

"It's me, your globetrotting friend. But I guess you have a lot of globetrotting friends?"

"I know a lot of globetrotting people, but I wouldn't call many of them friends," Ned replied, recognizing Tsu's voice.

"I won't ask what category I fall into," Tsu said. "Listen, your man, Chris Collins is in trouble."

"Oh, I *know* he's in trouble."

"SIA lists him as a target at the request of a group with international connections. Possibly involving your candidate Matthew McGoldrick, but I can't prove it yet."

"Thanks. I didn't know about SIA being onto him. I'll be sure to let him know he's even more screwed than he thought."

"Also, SIA will be transferring weapons to somebody at a disused tile factory on Mechra Lake east of Rabat on

December 10th. If you have anyone in the area, that's your window to intercept and capture."

"That's also great info. I'll pass it where it needs to go."

"Good. In return for all that, I need some help."

"Okay?"

"I'm in Morocco and I have nothing. Almost no money, and one set of torn up clothes. A dog even took some of my arm."

"Oh. Shit. What do you need? I can't get you a new arm but I might be able to help somehow."

"I'm heading to Rabat today. Weapons, clothes, money, and accommodation would all be very useful."

"I can't promise all of those, but I'll do my best. There's a hotel in Rabat that has the same name as a man you once killed in a very old city. Remember you told me once?"

"I remember."

"Someone will meet you there tonight. Good luck."

An hour later, Tsu was on a bus to Rabat. She covered her aching limbs, her mangled arm, and her whole face under a blanket, and slept.

33

A CLATTERING OF COINS

Through the contour-less farmland east of Lyon, Chris pushed the inadequate car as hard as he could, with Geneva in his sights.

As the engine began to complain harder, he left the farmland behind and plunged into forests, before crossing the rocky peaks of the Haute Chaîne du Jura national reserve. He was enjoying empty expanses of road where he didn't have to worry that somebody might be on his tail.

But roads without traffic began to disappear as he approached the Swiss border. He knew that the Swiss had abandoned customs checks at their land borders with the European Union, but his nervousness was growing nevertheless.

Even if the border caused no trouble, he knew there was trouble on the other side. He couldn't contact law enforcement. That was the last thing he wanted to do. He would have to try to protect Schneider from afar. Try to keep him alive. Alone.

Alone, except for Ned. Chris had tried to avoid contact, knowing that every call or message had the potential to land Ned in severe trouble. But Ned had now made the first move, and Chris's phone buzzed with a message.

Be aware: The SIA terrorist group lists you as a target.

Traffic was slowed to a halt as Chris reached the border, and he took the opportunity to reply.

Thanks, I'll add them to the list of people who want to kill me, he wrote. He hesitated, wondering if he should ask Ned for even more help. Then he told himself a man's life was at stake, and typed.

Walter Schneider is assassination target at upcoming UN crime convention. Contact Swiss authorities to up security, and let me know what you can about his regular locations. I owe you (again).

Glancing neither left nor right but only in his rearview mirror for any car that was looking too familiar, he drove over the border.

Geneva sits only a short distance from the border, and he was soon in the city. He checked himself into a cheap hotel in the Vernier district, then got to work.

It was dark when he stepped out of the hotel, but he wanted to have a look around the UN building. He knew Schneider wouldn't necessarily be targeted at the convention itself, and it might even happen a day or so earlier. But getting familiar with the area was important.

Then, Ned's message made him change direction:

Schneider attending a reception at British ambassador's residence tonight.

Chris nodded in approval of Ned's quick work as he read the message. Then, he had to make a quick plan himself, because hanging around outside a consulate at night wouldn't be easy. Especially when you look like a tramp.

Then it hit him. Why not *be* a tramp? His weeks on the run had prepared him perfectly for the role, now that he looked disheveled and beaten up. A scrawled sign begging for help, and he would be all set.

Within an hour, he was sitting on the cold, hard ground close to the British consulate. The street itself was polished and leafy, but the streets around it weren't particularly upmarket, and it wouldn't look odd to see homeless people in the area.

It was a bitterly cold night to be sitting still for hours on end, and Chris spared a thought for people who were forced by circumstance to do it every night.

Shortly before 8pm, a small motorcade arrived outside the consulate. Schneider stepped out of his car and stood briefly beneath the British flag as he looked up and down the street. Then, he stepped inside.

Chris wanted to get a look at the security detail. It seemed Schneider was taking some precautions, but not as many as he would be if he knew what Chris knew. One guy had gone inside the consulate with him, and one had now positioned himself outside the door. As Chris was trying to see if the guy was armed, a clattering of coins distracted him.

He looked up and saw an elderly woman nodding at him and smiling weakly as she threw some coins into the beanie hat in front of him.

But there weren't too many people around, and Chris was able to keep an eye on anybody who was on the street. Signs that somebody might be suspicious would be very subtle—as simple as a quick swivel of a phone towards the consulate to take a photo.

Two cold hours passed, and Chris saw nothing to alarm him. The woman who had given him money came back the opposite way, and smiled at him again. As she passed the consulate, she took a very brief glance at the guard on the doorstep.

He didn't know if it was instinct or experience, but something told Chris he had to follow. He waited until she was a good way down the street, then picked himself up off the floor.

Heading south, he followed her into a residential area with tower blocks in every direction. Keeping in the shadows, he stayed well behind as the woman entered a darkened park. She had been going at a fast pace for someone of her age, but now she slowed down.

Through the mist, Chris could just about see her as she stopped next to a metal trash can, then shoved in her hand and rummaged around. She moved on, out of the park and into another residential area.

Either this was a woman who gave coins to homeless people with one hand then rummaged through trash with another, or there was more to her than met the eye. Chris was certain he had just witnessed her picking up a dead drop: something left earlier in the agreed location by someone she was working with. The question was, what?

A few blocks down the street, she skipped up a short flight of stairs to the door of an apartment. Swiftly and quietly, Chris ran. Before she had taken her key from her purse, he was up behind her, placing his left hand over her mouth before she could even gasp. His right hand was holding his gun to her ribs.

"Open it," he whispered in her ear.

She opened the door and entered the cold apartment. She flicked on the lights to reveal a spartan room, the curtains faded by sunlight and the ceiling stained yellow by tobacco.

Even with his gun to her back, Chris was expecting a fight. He knew the old woman might not be old at all. She could be in disguise, and she could be highly trained.

"Hands on your head," he told her, searching her for weapons. He found none, but he removed a small package wrapped in plastic. He told her to sit down. She sat on the tatty sofa and faced him, her hands still on her head.

"Take off the wig," he told her. "Slowly."

She removed the gray wig, and long, blonde hair fell down around her shoulders. He could see she was maybe thirty-five years old, forty at the most. He could also see tears were streaming down her face.

"I'm going to do it," she said, her voice trembling. "I picked it up. I'll do it tomorrow."

"What did you pick up?"

"The toothpaste."

Chris paused. He could tell she was terrified. He had met some actors in his time, but if this woman was acting then she was one of the best.

"I'm not who you think I am," he told her. "I'm not working with whoever is running you."

The woman stared at him.

"Who are you?" she asked.

"I'm law enforcement. I can't tell you any more than that. What do they want you to do with the toothpaste?"

"If I tell you, they'll do terrible things to me. They've done it before."

"I'm going to get you out of this situation, but you need to help me. What are they asking you to do?"

The woman put her head in her hands, and sobbed.

"You need to tell me," Chris said. "They'll never let you go. They will never tell you you've done enough. You'll live your whole life in fear."

The woman took a deep breath.

"I work at the Beau-Rivage hotel. I'm a cleaner. A few months ago, someone approached me there. They said they knew I had been stealing from guest-rooms, and if I didn't do what they said they would tell the police."

"Had you been stealing?"

"Yes. That's how they get people. They find out things people have done wrong and they use it against them."

"Let me guess, they told you that you only had to do something small and they'd leave you alone?"

"Yes."

"But once you'd done it, there was something more you had to do. Then something more after that?"

"Yes," the woman said, her sobbing starting again. "A lot of important people stay at the hotel. Sometimes I just have to listen or watch. Sometimes worse. Before I knew it, I was doing much worse than stealing. I never stole a lot, just some cash or jewelry. Switzerland is expensive … sometimes I can't put the heating on."

"Do you have family?"

"Not in Geneva. I have kids back in Ukraine. I send back everything I earn."

"Good. It's good there's no one else involved. So what did they ask you to do this time?"

"They wanted me to put the toothpaste in some guy's room. A politician. I cleaned his room yesterday, checked what toothpaste he uses, then they told me to pick some up from the park today. I'm supposed to put it in his room when I start my shift tomorrow. It's got poison inside.

"Here's what we're going to do," Chris said. "An hour before you're supposed to start your shift, you're going to call your handler. You're going to tell him that you're having doubts and you don't know if you can go through with it."

"I can't do that."

"Yes, you can. You need to say you're in Bourg du Four square, you have been drinking and your head is all over the place. He'll come to meet you."

"Please, I don't want to see him."

"You won't. By the time he gets there, you'll be a long way from Geneva. You'll be on a train out of Switzerland. I'll be meeting him at the square, so you'll need to tell me what he looks like."

"Okay," the woman said softly. She seemed to have calmed a little.

"There's one more thing you'll need to do. When he realizes you're not at the square, he will try calling you. Just tell him you're not going to do what they ask any more, in fact you already called the police a few days ago. Don't say anything more, just hang up. Now, you need to pack your things, because you won't be coming back to Geneva."

AN HOUR LATER, Chris and the woman were standing at Genève-Cornavin railway station.

"Someone will meet you at the other end. Tell them your name is Julia," Chris said. After making sure the woman got on the train, he typed a message to Ned.

Get somebody to meet a woman, 35-40 yo with blonde hair, off the Geneva-Stuttgart train arriving 14:35. Name Julia. Needs asset protection.

Then, he headed to Bourg-de-Four square. It was morning rush hour and the square was hectic, which made it difficult to pick out individuals. But Chris needed the crowds to help him get close to the handler without being noticed.

He scanned the square many times, until just after 8:30 when he spotted the man he was looking for: heavy set with slicked-back hair and, most tellingly, looking for someone who wasn't there.

Immediately, Chris was on the move. He walked up

behind the guy, deftly dropped a listening device into his pocket, and was away.

He leant slightly behind a stone statue, pretended to be engrossed in his phone, and put in an earpiece while keeping an eye on the man. After turning around to observe the square a few times, the man took out his phone.

Chris couldn't hear the conversation, but he saw anger on the man's face. He hoped that meant the woman had done as instructed. But he couldn't figure out why he wasn't hearing anything.

The man was on the move, and Chris followed, picking his way through office workers, tourists, and cyclists. He followed the guy as he crossed the University of Geneva campus, then saw him stop beside a car. The man took a quick look left and right, then got in.

Chris ducked down a side street then turned his head back to look at the car. The guy was taking out his phone, and Chris could hear the dialing tone, his listening device suddenly working loud and clear.

"The fucking bitch has bailed on us," the man said in French. "... I don't know; she said she was having doubts."

A pause.

"It's too late for that. She already told the police everything. A few days ago."

Another pause.

"I don't know what they know, or who they have been following. But if they know about Rabat then everything's ruined. We won't get a chance to take out high-level Americans for a very long time."

Chris's mind was racing as he processed what he was hearing, and the man kept talking.

"They'll definitely know about Schneider, that will have to be pulled. But Rabat could still be a go. I'll ask my contact at Fedpol, find out what they know. In the meantime, let's get info on anyone she has been seen with in the last few days."

The sound of an engine entered Chris's earpiece, and he turned to see the car driving away, taking the listening device out of range.

His priority now was to get out of Geneva, and to stop whatever was going to happen in Rabat. He took out his phone, ready to send another message to Ned. But Ned still hadn't replied to the one requesting help for the woman on the train out of Switzerland. More than two hours, and nothing. Chris was trying not to worry, but for Ned, such a lack of response was highly unusual.

34

ARRIVED

Six hours after he had been in Bourg-de-Foursquare, Chris was heading east into the heart of Switzerland. Just driving.

The group McGoldrick was working for seemed to have operators everywhere. They had sent someone for him in Bordeaux, and they were clearly in Geneva too. McGoldrick's link to Basem hinted at a North African connection, and so did the Rabat plot. Whatever that involved.

The countryside felt like the right place to be. They might have tracked him down to Bordeaux, or they could just have had eyes on Marianne. Geneva was a major location for the UN. But if they were in every sleepy Swiss town and on every mountainside, then something truly terrifying was going on.

Pine-forested hills were getting fewer and the mountain peaks were becoming more jagged. Driving on, Chris took out his phone and looked for a message from

Ned. Nothing. He felt terrible for dragging his good friend into this mess. For dragging his wife, and maybe even the whole of the CIA into it too.

He couldn't wait any longer. He decided to do something he wouldn't have dreamed of doing just a week ago. He had to call Helen.

He didn't allow himself time for doubt. He dialed her personal number, which had been etched in his memory for years.

"Helen Miller."

"Helen. It's Chris."

Silence. Then Helen said:

"Where are you?"

"I can't tell you that, but I have to tell you something. There's a plot to kill Americans in Morocco. Rabat. Multiple Americans, some high-level, possibly their families too. It's a group McGoldrick is involved with. I don't know what exactly his role is or who the group is, but they have international connections and were targeting Walter Schneider in Geneva. Watch McGoldrick, and watch Rabat."

"Okay, Chris. Thank you, I know it must have been a hard choice to contact me."

"It was, and now I need to go."

"Chris, wait," Helen said. "We know about McGoldrick. We don't know exactly what he's up to, but we know it's something. And we know he tried to set you up."

Chris was briefly silent. Shocked.

"How did you find out?" he asked.

"We were onto the Schneider plot too, and now we know McGoldrick is connected to it. I'm sorry I doubted you. But I can help you now. Where are you?"

Amazed, Chris tried to quickly assess what he needed most.

"Switzerland," he said. North of Montreux. Can you get me a safe house?"

"Of course. Are you being followed?"

"I don't think so. But it's possible the group knows I was in Geneva. I just got out of there."

"Good. I'll get back to you on this number with a safe house."

Chris was hit with a surge of emotion. Whether Helen would have helped him if she didn't know about McGoldrick, he had no idea. But the important thing is that she had helped him. After the past weeks he had spent alone, it was good just to speak to a friend.

If he could get out of Europe without being found by the group, he might even be able to investigate what was going on in Morocco in an official capacity, and help to stop the attack.

He checked himself and made sure to focus on the task in hand. To get out of Switzerland alive.

As he drove over a mountain pass with breathtaking valleys beneath him, his phone buzzed.

A village called Oberwil, in the mountains south of Bern. Follow signs for Gantrisch Nature Park then join Route 11, it runs right through. Call me when arrived for final details. H.

He wanted to ask about Ned in his reply, but he didn't want to even mention his name to Helen. She was so straight-laced she might even punish Ned for helping a rogue agent that had a very good reason to be rogue.

He pushed thoughts that Ned had already been rumbled to the back of his mind. He needed to keep himself alive, then he could argue Ned's case later.

He slowly descended out of the mountains and towards Gantrisch Nature Park, noticing signs for the road he needed. Two hours later, he was in Oberwil.

He pulled over next to a serene village green and sent a message to Helen.

Arrived.

The reply came back within seconds.

Drive west out of the village, white farmhouse with blue window shutters. Knock twice and ask which way to the train station.

Chris drove less than a mile before he saw the farmhouse. He found somewhere to leave his car out of sight of the road, then walked up to the door. He knocked on it twice.

A woman spoke from behind the door.

"Ja?"

"I'm looking for the train station. Could you tell me where it is?"

The door opened.

Standing before Chris was a short woman in her late forties, her cheeks flushed with red veins. She smiled and gestured for Chris to come in.

Inside the farmhouse, he walked into a kitchen with a terracotta tiled floor and a beautiful oak table that reminded him of his own back home.

Sitting at the table was a man with cheeks equally as flushed as the woman's. In front of him was an unlabeled bottle of red wine.

"Made it!" the man said, grinning at Chris. He picked up a fresh glass.

What a surprise, Chris thought. *Someone is gonna ask me to drink with them.*

Within an hour, they had raced through a bottle each. Even by the standards of everybody else who had roped him into a drinking session, this couple could really drink.

Using a mix of French, German, and English, the three of them were soon into tails of adventure. The couple, Luca and Ana, explained that they had met Helen while working for French intelligence, when Helen had been stationed in Paris for a while.

Now, aside from the occasional bit of help offered to people they had done important work with in the past, they were out of the game. They had found a farm in a quiet village, and taken themselves away from everything.

The sun had barely set outside the window, but Chris's head was spinning. The stress and trauma of the past few weeks, plus the speed at which this couple drank the strong wine, was getting to him. It could be the first time in years that somebody outdrank him.

Luca decided this was the right time to bring out the good stuff. He pulled himself out of his seat, waved his hand at Chris as if telling him to wait, and then disappeared to the pantry.

Chris could hear him rattling around, and he soon emerged with what seemed to be a full pig hidden under a cloth. In his other hand he had a tray with three glasses of murky brown liquid.

"Homemade brandy," he announced. "Sensational with ham."

He placed a glass down in front of Chris and removed the cloth from the huge ham, preparing to cut a slice.

Chris went to raise his glass in thanks for their hospitality, but he fumbled and it slipped through his hands, tipping onto its side and spilling brandy across the table.

"Oh, shit," he said, turning to Ana to ask for a towel. There was a look of pure hatred in her eyes. He turned to see Luca was also staring him hard.

He was about to apologize for wasting the homemade brandy when he saw Ana's hand on the carving knife.

Through his drunken haze, he reacted just quickly enough, jumping to his feet as she came at him with the knife. He dodged her wild swing and leapt back.

She was coming at him again, but he managed to chop at her forearm, making her drop the knife.

He sensed Luca bearing down on him from the left, and swung his right elbow as he turned, crashing it into Luca's neck.

Luca stayed on his feet and came back with a left hook. Chris swerved but the punch connected, rattling his brain. He opened his eyes to see Ana picking up the knife and turning towards him, her teeth gritted with rage.

He grabbed a wine bottle from the table, knowing he had the longer reach. As the woman approached him, he swung the bottle and collided with her head, a mixture of reds spraying into the air as her face was cut open.

As she slumped to the ground, he turned back towards Luca ... but was too late. The man landed a vicious headbutt between Chris's eyes, making him stumble back into a wall. Luca delivered another headbutt that left Chris reeling.

He could feel Luca's hands on his throat. The guy had a strong grip, and Chris felt the panic of being choked. He knew he would lose consciousness very quickly.

In a purely instinctive move, he pulled Luca towards him, making him lean forwards. He swung his left knee upwards, crunching it into Luca's body right under his ribcage.

The grip was loosened as Luca's body dealt with the blow, and Chris took his chance. He hit Luca with three quick and fierce right hands, sending him to the floor. Then, he looked around for the knife.

It was on the stone floor a meter away from Ana, who was trying to get up off her knees. But she was in an awful, bloodied state.

Chris steeled himself for what he was about to do. He strode over and picked up the knife. Then, without hesitation, he knelt beside Ana. He picked up her head, put the knife to her neck, and opened her throat in one cut.

Luca was on his belly, trying to lift himself. But he barely had time to struggle as Chris stepped to him and sliced his neck open. Chris let go of the man's hair and his head crashed to the ground.

Breathing hard, Chris looked at his bloodied hands. He turned to see the spilled brandy that he now realized must have contained poison. Then, he stared at the dead bodies on the floor.

He searched pockets, but found nothing. Scanning the room, he saw Ana's purse on a coat stand. He grabbed it and opened it up. He pocketed a handful of euro notes, then picked up a phone.

In the phone was one anonymous contact—their number prefixed with a United States dialing code—and a single text message:

He can fight. Use subtle methods.

Chris felt sick knowing who the message was from. With hatred and anger coursing through him, he replied.

It's done.

35

SOMEONE YOU KNOW

S tanding in the farmhouse kitchen with bodies at his feet, Chris ripped off his blood-stained shirt. He ran upstairs, searching quickly for clean clothes, and found one of Luca's shirts that was a little tight but would do the job.

A minute later, he was in the car and back on the road. He zipped along country roads in any direction that would let him move most freely.

His head was scrambled. If Helen was a traitor—working with the same group as McGoldrick—who else might be? The only person he still trusted wasn't replying to his messages, and he didn't even know if Ned was still in possession of his phone.

He drove on through the night towards the Italian border. As he ran through his mind everything Helen had ever said to him, and whether he should have picked something up, his phone buzzed with a message:

Everything is FUBAR.

Chris stared at the message. Was it really Ned, or someone using Ned's phone to bait a reply? Another message followed:

More FUBAR than the Battle of Adrianople. No idea what that is but you mentioned it once when we were supposed to be talking about women.

Chris smiled. He tapped in a reply.

Yes, everything is. Helen is working with McGoldrick.

Ned's response came quickly.

Oh. Shit. That's a new definition of the acronym.

Are you in trouble? Chris asked.

Agency know I have been helping you. Now trying to leave the country.

I'm sorry I dragged you into this. Stay calm, think straight and you'll be fine. I'm heading to Rabat. Attack on Americans imminent.

I'll try. I guess my help ends here but I do have a contact in Rabat who can help you. Head for the Hotel Laszlo.

Is it someone I can trust?

It's someone you know. Smart, beautiful, and extremely useful.

I think I know who you mean. Thanks.

Good luck.

Chris was driving on, trying to decide on his next move, when a signpost helped him to decide. It said Milan Malpensa Airport was only ninety kilometers away. Without knowing who to rely on for help, he had to get to Rabat and try to stop the attack. For that, he was willing to risk using his false passport and trying to board a plane.

Within an hour he was driving along the shore of Lake Como across the Italian border, heading south towards Milan.

Two hours later, he had ditched his car and his gun, and was standing in line at Malpensa. Burly airport security staff, who looked like they worked out tons and ate even more, were holding machine guns like they couldn't wait to use them.

But the guy who checked Chris's passport looked like he couldn't wait to clock off and take a nap. Soon, Chris was on a plane that was taxiing, turning its nose towards Rabat.

36

I NEED A WEAPON

Found in Rabat's Medina, the ancient walled city encircled by the bustling modern day capital, Hotel Laszlo was set in an exquisite 17th-century townhouse.

Chris walked into the hotel through its central courtyard that was covered in ornate blue-and-green tiles and had trickling fountains dotted around it.

Through elegant stone archways, he saw bottles glistening behind a bar. Evening was arriving, and he felt a drink would help him think.

Great, looks like being on the run has turned me into an alcoholic, he thought as he approached the bar.

His heart sang as he noticed a bottle of Glenlivet, and he ordered a double. He swirled the delightful brown liquid around in the glass as he forced his brain to think about what the target might be. But the glass was empty and no answer had presented itself, so he ordered another Scotch.

I'll take one of those, a woman's voice said behind him, and he turned to look. His eyes met Tsu's, and they both smiled fondly.

"Let's move away from the bar," Chris said when Tsu had been served her Scotch.

"It's good to see a friendly face," Tsu said as they took a seat in a quiet corner. "I've had a crazy few weeks."

"Likewise," Chris said. "It seems like the whole world has gone crazy."

"Thank God for Scotch!" Tsu said, tipping her glass to admire the tones. "This is a great one."

"It's my favorite," Chris told her. "Has been for a long while."

"I think it might be mine from now on," Tsu said, then added: "Here's to Ned, for bringing us together again." They clinked.

"To Ned," Chris agreed. "I don't know how he does it."

"Me neither! I told him I needed some help in Rabat, the next thing I know, somebody walks up to me in the bar here, hands me a bag with everything I could possibly need, then walks off without saying a word."

"He did the same for me in Bordeaux. Incredible. I won't ask you how you know him, because I know from experience you won't tell me. Even he wouldn't tell me. If you ask him to keep something secret, he always will."

"I'll tell you more about myself one day, I promise," Tsu said. "But there are more urgent things we need to discuss first."

"Agreed," Chris replied.

"One thing I do need to tell you right now: the SIA group have you as a target."

"Thanks, I know. Ned informed me. The number of people trying to kill me is growing by the day."

"I started an operation in Yangon not long ago, and since then I have made nothing but enemies."

"Who do you think is after you?"

"I was investigating illegal arms trading, but it's grown much bigger than that. There's an international group planning an attack, and SIA are supplying the weapons. I've identified some of the individuals involved, all of different nationalities, but I don't know when or where the attack is."

Chris felt a rush of adrenaline, knowing that Tsu had her claws into the same conspiracy he had been tracking. It would be so good to have her by his side.

"It sounds like we ended up in Rabat for the same reasons," he told Tsu. "The attack is right here in the city, but I don't know precisely where. I do know that high-level Americans are among the targets."

"We might not know the target location, but I know where the weapons exchange will be. If we can stop that, we can cut them off at the source," Tsu said.

"That's perfect," Chris said. "We can stop the weapons before they even get to the target. Where's the exchange?"

"So you'll help me?" Tsu asked.

"Of course!"

"That's so good to hear," Tsu said, staring into Chris's eyes. "Thank you."

"You were there for me in Cuba," he replied. "It's the least I could do."

"If taking on terrorists is the least you can do, I would love to see the most you can do!"

Right then, a group of two couples walked into the bar, chatting noisily.

"I don't think this is the right place to make a plan," Tsu said. "How about we go up to my room. It's a suite, there's plenty of space."

"A suite? That Ned got you?" Chris asked. "I was pretty happy with my last care package, but now I'm starting to change my mind."

THE SUITE in the historic townhouse retained all the charm of years gone by. Warm red fabrics had been worked into the artisan rugs and plush sofas that were positioned around the fireplace. The room was lit by soft light flickering from behind wrought iron lamps.

"If I ever get to a point in my life where people stop trying to kill or arrest me," Chris said, looking into his whiskey glass, "I'm going to do a tour of the Scottish Highlands, and visit as many distilleries as I can."

"That sounds incredible," Tsu replied. "If people stop trying to kill me, I'd love to do the same thing. Why didn't I choose to become a master distiller, instead of … this?"

"That would have been a very good choice of occupation. I guess you'll just have to make do with drinking the stuff."

"We're supposed to be planning," Tsu said, her lips curling into a smile as she looked at Chris.

"Yeah."

They were both silent for a moment, trying to transition from the peaceful moment to the dangerous job in hand.

"The exchange will take place two days from now," Tsu said. "A deserted factory next to a lake east of the city."

"The weapons must be small," Chris said. "Anything big would be too risky to move around a city like Rabat. And they will be keeping the number of people involved in the exchange to a minimum. I hope. But we still have a major problem: there are only two of us, and I for one have no weapons."

"Ned's guy brought me a Beretta pistol. Only one though."

"I had to ditch mine before I got on a plane in Milan. It will be difficult to stop the exchange on our own, but it's too risky to alert the Moroccan authorities at this stage. There could be someone on the inside who will tip off the group that the exchange point is compromised, and they will move it elsewhere."

"I agree. If it's too dangerous for us to try to stop the exchange, we can at least follow the collectors and try to get help later."

"The important thing is that we're there at the point of exchange, and that we can move fast if we need to."

"We have two days," Tsu said. "We need to get some motorcycles … "

"Right. And I need a weapon. A firearm will be impossible, but maybe some kind of blade."

Tsu placed her whiskey tumbler on the table in front of her, and walked into the bedroom. When she came back, she was holding something covered with cloth."

"Will this do?" she asked, peeling back the cloth to reveal the most beautiful dagger Chris had ever seen."

"Wow," he said. "It's going to be a shame for that thing to be covered in blood."

"Well, unless you can kindly persuade the terrorists to change their ways, this thing will have to get wet."

37

SAFETY OFF

C hris and Tsu were crouching on a dusty concrete floor. The sound of leaking water slowly dripping onto a metal drum was echoing around the huge, dark factory. They were silent. Waiting.

Then, Tsu spoke:

"The ideal scenario is a few quick shots that take them all out." she whispered, reiterating the plan. "Failing that, it might have to be hand-to-hand. Last resort is we decide we can't take them on, and we try to follow whoever collected the weapons."

"Agreed," Chris replied. "If we can get it over with right here and now, let's do it."

A few minutes later, the sound of a distant engine put them on high alert. It was getting closer.

As they had predicted after checking out the factory, a vehicle—a black SUV—entered through the large cargo doors that led into the vast hall in the center of the building. The vehicle rumbled to a halt. Nobody stepped out.

Five minutes later, the sound of smaller engines could be heard outside. Two motorcycles entered the factory. There was a man on each bike, but only one of them was carrying a backpack. They cut the engines and stepped off.

"SIA," Tsu whispered.

Two men emerged from the SUV, dressed more smartly, in perfectly tailored suits. Without a word, the backpack was handed over.

Slowly, Tsu clicked the safety off her gun. From behind the drum that was shielding her, she had a clear line of sight to all four men. She would have to be fast.

"Good luck," Chris whispered.

Holding the gun in her right hand and resting it on her left for stability, she took aim. Her heart racing but her hands perfectly steady, she pulled the trigger.

Flames filled the air as a giant explosion threw Chris and Tsu across the room. They landed with crunching thuds ten meters from where they had been crouching.

Chris found himself staring up at the metal pipes on the ceiling way above him. He lay still for a few seconds, breathing hard. Then he turned to look for Tsu.

She was already on her feet, but her head was bleeding heavily. Chris leapt to his feet and followed her as she began firing. One of the four men was disappearing round the back of the SUV, and Tsu's third shot ricocheted off the vehicle, just missing him.

Tsu and Chris took cover behind a stack of metal pallets, crouching low.

"What the hell was that?" Tsu whispered.

"I'm guessing whatever was leaking wasn't water," Chris said. "And the gunshot sparked it."

They turned to see the two men in suits getting onto the motorcycle, one of them now carrying the backpack. There was no sign of the two terrorists who had arrived on the bikes. Tsu took aim.

"No, it's too dangerous," Chris said, putting his hand on her arm. We need to follow them."

They stood to move towards their own bikes, but a heavy blow crashed hard into Tsu's head, staggering her.

Chris saw that the two terrorists were right on them, both holding knives. The man on the left took a swing at Chris, but he swerved and dodged it.

"Who are you?" the man shouted. "Why are you here?"

"Screw you," Chris said.

Both men now raised their knives. Chris went to move himself between them and Tsu, who was in a daze. The men stepped forward, their weapons out in front of them.

Chris felt around his hip for the dagger, but it was gone. He realized he must have lost in when he fell.

The men moved fast, jabbing at him with the knives as he dodged. He was trying to get a blow on a forearm to make at least one of them drop a weapon. But they were well trained.

He was slipping their murderous jabs, but they were

gradually moving him into a corner. From there, he would have no way to escape.

His eyes were fixed on the rusty blades when he saw something flying past his head. Tsu's black boot smashed into the face of the man closest to Chris. There was a sickening crunch as the terrorist's head snapped back, and he slumped to the ground. Chris was sure Tsu had killed him with one kick.

The other man looked momentarily shocked at what had happened, then turned his attention to Tsu. His teeth gritted, he lunged at Tsu with his knife, but Chris came in with a right cross and landed on the jaw.

Tsu tried to get the man into a chokehold while he was stunned, but he was strong and he threw her off, sending her onto her back and skidding across the floor.

Chris took his chance and grabbed the knife-wielding hand. But the terrorist was an experienced fighter, and he used quick-fire punches to take back control. Chris countered with blows of his own, but it would only take a split-second for the knife to get through and end Chris's life right there and then.

As he took a step back to go again, he saw Tsu over the man's shoulder. She had picked up the beautiful dagger and was ready to slide it across the floor.

Chris nodded, and the dagger came skidding towards his feet. At the same time, Tsu approached the terrorist from behind. She spun and released a brutal kick into his spine, making him tip his head back as he yelled out in pain.

In one move, Chris grabbed the dagger from off the

floor and arced it towards the man's neck. He opened the terrorist's throat, the blood flooding over the blade of the dagger.

Chris and Tsu exchanged glances for just a moment, then moved to get out of the factory. But the noise of sirens approached at high speed, and in seconds police vehicles had surrounded the building.

Tsu gestured to Chris that she knew a way out. But as they turned to go, they saw multiple guns trained on them and heard an officer shouting at them through a megaphone in Arabic. They raised their hands, and put them on their heads. There was no other choice.

38

NO COINCIDENCE

C hris stood from the hard wooden bench of the jail cell and paced the tiny room. He had spent weeks on the run from prosecution for a fabricated crime, and now he had been arrested for a crime he had truly committed.

No matter what explanation he gave, the fact remained that when he was found by police, he was standing over two dead bodies.

Along with Tsu, whose voice he could hear a few cells down the corridor, he had tried to explain that there was an attack imminent in Rabat. But they had both just been told to shut up.

It seemed impossible to talk his way out of the cell. He thought about how the CIA wouldn't have helped him out of this kind of situation even when he was working for them. He always knew he might end up like this. But a Moroccan prison was not a place anyone could face spending the rest of their lives.

He stared at the damp concrete walls for hours. Finally, he dropped to sleep.

When he awoke, it was because he could hear Tsu's raised voice. She was arguing with one of the guards, the noisy discussion going around in circles, and the word "phone call" cropping up regularly during a conversation that mixed Arabic, English, and French.

Then, Chris heard the clanking of a door being opened.

"Holy hell, okay. Phone call!" the guard yelled, clearly having lost his temper. "One minute. Stand there, I listen. Then you shut up."

Chris then heard Tsu speaking on the phone in a language he was pretty sure was Korean, but he couldn't understand what was being said.

"Hey!" the guard yelled. "What's this language!"

Tsu spoke fast, clearly making sure she got out as much information as possible. A few seconds later, Chris heard more arguing followed by a scuffle. He then heard Tsu cursing the guard as her cell door was slammed shut.

A few hours later, Tsu was lying awake in the darkness. Aside from occasional angry, desperate shouts from prisoners, the place was silent.

Then, suddenly, Tsu heard her door being opened, the bolt clanking loudly. The guard she had been arguing with earlier was standing there.

"You are leaving," he told her, to her extreme surprise.

Without questioning it, she stood from the bench and followed him.

"A powerful man said you can go, so you can go," the guard told her as he booked her out and handed her her things. Then, he looked over her shoulder and nodded at somebody.

She turned and saw a face she would never have believed she could see there. Osman.

"Let's go," he said bluntly. Tsu hesitated. So Osman took out his ID and showed it to her. "I'm Moroccan secret service," he said. "I was undercover in Bamako. Now, let's get going before I change my mind."

"My friend is also here," Tsu explained.

"I know. They told me you were arrested together. He's coming too."

Chris appeared across the room, looking confused.

Tsu shrugged.

"He's getting us out. Better than life in prison, that's for sure,"

Osman led the way out, with Tsu and Chris following behind.

"Is this the guy you called?" Chris asked.

"No! He's a guy I was tracking in Bamako. But it turns out he was undercover, Moroccan secret service."

Chris puffed out his cheeks and exhaled as he processed the information.

Outside the station, the first rays of dawn were creeping over the horizon as a burly agent with an earpiece opened a car door for Chris and Tsu. Osman was already inside.

"How did you know I was here?" Tsu asked.

"I had my suspicions about you in Bamako," Osman

explained. "When a beautiful woman is immediately friendly, spies always have their suspicions. When you were captured at the farmhouse I looked into you. Then I heard about the incident at the factory, and someone with your description. It didn't take much working out."

"Well," Tsu said. "Thank you for getting me out. Getting *us* out."

"We're on the same side. You, I, and Mr Collins. I have great respect for you, sir, and your time as CIA Deputy Director. And, now, I'm sure you were framed. We have been watching McGoldrick for a while. Unfortunately, we passed our concerns onto your Director, Helen Miller, who failed to act on them."

"That's because she's with McGoldrick," Chris explained.

Osman was silent for a moment.

"That is very, very troubling," he said. "It explains a few things, but it's deeply concerning. It frightens me to wonder who is involved in this conspiracy and how high up it goes. We haven't found enough evidence on McGoldrick to bring him in, and nobody seems willing to even criticize him."

Tsu then interrupted.

"Whoever is involved in all this, the one thing we do know is that an attack in Rabat is imminent. Weapons were exchanged at the factory and we believe they were for an attack in the city."

"That's also our assessment," Osman said. "And there's something else you need to know. McGoldrick just landed in Rabat. He's attending a private event at the

Palm Sands Golf Resort. It has all been kept very much on the down-low but we have known about it for a while. It can't be a coincidence."

"So you'll have people on the ground?" Chris asked.

"We'll have eyes on him at the resort hotel and plenty of security," Osman confirmed. "He thinks the security is for him, but actually it's there in case he tries anything."

"When is the event?" Tsu asked.

"Lunchtime today. And I'm going to need your help."

39

DO YOU COPY?

I n a large storeroom within the Palm Sands hotel, Osman was explaining his plan.

"I've designated this as a safe room," he told Chris and Tsu. "It has a heavy door and only one way in and out. If there are shooters in the building, we direct people here and barricade them in. It's not ideal, but at least we all know where to head to if we need to protect people."

Chris and Tsu took a look around the room, memorizing its layout.

"Chris, you should stay here," Osman said. "We need someone with your experience to keep people calm and tell them how to proceed."

"That's not going to happen," Chris replied. "I need to know as soon as an attack starts, not only help people who are running from it."

"Sir, as I said, I respect your credentials. But I am running the show here."

"We're here to help, not take orders," Chris said, looking Osman in the eye. "I'm not just going to sit here and wait."

Osman looked angry, but backed down.

"Well, wherever you want to position yourself, you need to make sure McGoldrick doesn't see you."

"Of course," Chris replied.

"One of us has to be in the room with McGoldrick," Tsu said. "He has obviously planned to bring the target or targets together in a place where they can be hit. I suspect that is his main role: only somebody of his standing could arrange for high-level people to be in a certain place at a certain time."

"Agreed," Osman said.

"I'll get into the room, somehow," Tsu told him. "I'll keep an eye on what's happening in there."

"Good," Osman replied. "I'll watch the perimeter outside. I have security team out there." He handed out two-way radios and earpieces. "Channel 8," he said. Then, without another word, he handed them each a pistol.

Thirty minutes later, Tsu had been shopping. She had noticed some of the female staff were wearing headscarves, and she found one among the hotel's many shops. She had also noticed that the uniform of catering staff seemed to be a classic white blouse and black pants, which she had also managed to purchase. In the hotel's boutique stores they were actually expensive designer items, but from a distance it would be hard to tell the difference.

As she was changing into her new clothes in one of the hotel's public toilets, her receiver crackled.

"More details on the gathering," Osman said. "It's a reception for the American ambassador to Morocco, Sam Wharton, thrown by McGoldrick. Supposedly to thank him for his service before he moves to another post. The ambassador is the target but note that his wife and young family will be attending. Two children will be in the room, a boy and a girl under the age of ten."

"Motherfucker," Tsu hissed down the receiver.

"Indeed," Osman replied. "Let's get this piece of shit."

"Copy that."

"The reception begins in one hour in the main ballroom. What's your plan?"

"To look as much like catering staff as possible."

"Good. There will be plenty of trays being passed around before lunch, just grab one and stay in place."

"Copy."

While they had been talking, Chris had been crawling on his hands and knees. He was positioned on a maintenance walkway above the dropped ceiling, among wiring and large pipes.

"Mr Collins, do you copy?"

"Copy. In position above the ballroom."

Osman paused, then decided he didn't have time to ask how Chris already knew the location. In fact, Chris had figured out that McGoldrick would want the best venue in the place. He'd even want to superficially impress the people he was about to kill, that's how self-obsessed he was.

"Copy," Osman said. "Do you have eyes on the room?"

"Almost all of it. And when something happens, these tiles can be kicked out in seconds. With any luck, I'll be able to break McGoldrick's neck as I pass him on the way down."

"Copy. Over and out."

A short time later as the reception was getting underway, Tsu slyly picked up a tray of drinks and began circulating the room. There were other dignitaries in attendance — most of them were probably unfortunate collateral, Tsu thought, but possibly some were people who could stand in the way of whatever McGoldrick was planning and were supposed to be there. Decent people who happened to be standing in the way of someone's plan.

She looked across the spacious hall towards where McGoldrick was greeting guests. She watched as the ambassador arrived, a square-shouldered man with a warm smile. McGoldrick smiled back as he shook Wharton's hand, then crouched to talk to the children. Tsu felt her stomach tighten with anger.

There were the usual pleasantries as people mingled and chatted, but adrenaline was now flowing through Tsu's body because she knew the attack could come at any time.

As she picked her way around the room, a huge crash made her spin around to look at the far end of the hall.

Cutlery was flying through the air, and she whipped her spare hand towards her gun.

Then, she realized what happened. A waiter had dropped a tray, sending its contents into the air. She glanced around the room and then towards McGoldrick to make sure nobody had spotted her reaction. McGoldrick still wore a fixed smile.

As she circulated, Tsu was wondering if she should find some way to get the children out right now. If she took them elsewhere, away from the ambassador, it was less likely they would be caught up in the attack.

Then, the bullets came. The gunshots were far enough away that at first they didn't even get the attention of the guests, but they soon came loud and fast. When the glass from an exterior window exploded into the hall, panic set in.

There were shrieks of terror as people covered their heads, not knowing if they should run or get to the ground. Tsu drew her gun and fired towards the window, then made her way towards the young boy and girl.

Shots were coming thick and fast, but she couldn't see any gunmen. She grabbed a guard from the security detail, hoping Osman had briefed him on who she was and what the plan would be.

"We need to get these kids to the safe room," she shouted over the noise of gunfire. The man nodded, and they went to where the ambassador and his wife where huddling around their children. The room was now in chaos with people running for the exits. McGoldrick was nowhere to be seen.

"This way!" the guard shouted, leading the ambassador, his family, and any other people they could get to pay attention out the back of the room.

As the sound of gunshots and chaos continued nearby, they made their way down winding corridors towards the safe room,

Finally, they reached it, and Tsu ushered everyone inside.

"I'll come back for you when the gunmen are dealt with," the guard said, before closing the door and heading back to join the fight.

The ambassador's daughter was hysterical, and her parents seemed too shell-shocked to comfort her.

Tsu knelt down in front of her and spoke softly.

"It will be okay, we're safe now," she told the girl. "What's your name?"

The girl looked into Tsu's eyes while still whimpering.

"I'm Lisa," Tsu continued. "What's your name?"

"Sophia," the girl said quietly.

"It's lovely to meet you, Sophia," Tsu said, smiling. The girl smiled back. "How old are you?"

"Nine."

"I remember when I was nine, I was scared of everything. Now, I'm not scared of anything."

The conversation was interrupted by the crackling of Tsu's receiver.

"Is everyone okay?" Osman asked down the line.

"Shaken up, but no injuries," Tsu confirmed.

"Good. We're getting things under control out here. But stay there until I give the all clear."

"Copy that."

Tsu turned to the room.

"We're going to be fine," she said. "We just need to stay here a while longer until … "

She was interrupted by heavy coughing from the ambassador's son, followed by coughing from several others. Then, the room went black.

Standing in the darkness, Tsu could smell a faint scent of gas. Fear gripped her as she realized what was happening. Deadly hydrogen cyanide was being released into the room.

She ran for the door and pulled hard, but it didn't move.

"Open the door!" the ambassador yelled over the sound of screaming and coughing.

"The lock is electric and the power is out," Tsu shouted back. "Get on the floor, and cover your face with your clothes."

She made sure everybody was as low to the ground as they could be and had covered their faces, then she tried to calm the children. But she knew that in just a few minutes, they would all be dead.

40

RELEASE THE GAS

Crouching above the ceiling, Chris watched from above as Osman stood below him in the hotel's electrical room, adjacent to the ballroom, and cut the power. He now knew that Osman had tricked them, and that the bullets in the guns he had given were blanks.

He could see Osman had his own gun tucked into his belt. With little time to think, he made his decision. He pulled a tile out of the ceiling and dropped down, crashing his left elbow into Osman's neck as he landed. With his right hand, he went for the gun and got his fingers around the handle, but Osman was already fighting back.

He swung his whole body to throw Chris off, and the gun slipped from Chris's hand. It skidded across the floor and under an electrical unit. The men were now engaged in hand-to-hand combat.

Osman fought hard and fast, throwing hooked elbows and following up with fists. Chris was quick enough to block a lot of the shots, but he had to find a way to get on the attack. He took one step back, giving himself enough room to land a powerful kick in Osman's abdomen that sent him hurtling backwards into a wall.

As the two adversaries stared at each other, Chris's receiver crackled. Tsu's panicked voice came through.

"Chris! We're trapped and the door won't open," she said between violent coughs. "You need to turn on the power. They're pumping gas in here!"

"You were supposed to be in there as well," Osman growled.

Chris ignored him and moved towards the switchboard, looking for the switch that would turn the power back on in the room where he knew Tsu was trapped.

But Osman was back at him, maneuvering himself to Chris's side and bringing his knee around to land a vicious blow at the bottom of Chris's spine. Stunned, Chris fell back onto the switchboard, and Osman was towering over him.

With his left arm trapped underneath him, it was difficult for Chris to defend himself. Osman delivered two quick strikes to the ribs, then went for the throat. He could feel the rough skin on Osman's palm as the hand began to close around his neck. He thought about the people in the room where Tsu was, their lives ebbing away.

As Osman began to squeeze, Chris used all of his experience to keep his mind clear and his thoughts straight. He reached down towards his waist with his right hand, fumbling around for the gun. It was trapped between his body and the machinery, but he managed to clasp his fingers around the handle, shifting his body weight as he pulled the gun out.

He whipped it up and shoved the muzzle into Osman's eye. He fired. The explosion of the blank blasted Osman's head back, making him howl in pain. As the weight was lifted off Chris, he saw Osman's left eye had been totally destroyed.

Before Osman had even fallen to the ground, Chris had turned and was looking at the switchboard. There were dials and switches everywhere, and the labels were in Arabic. He was used to staying calm when he needed to save his own life, but knowing that others would die painful deaths, including Tsu, sent terror through his body. He breathed deep.

Then, he saw a row of switches that all sat below green lights, except one. That was below a red light. Immediately, Chris hammered the switch and the light turned green.

He got on the receiver and pushed down on the button.

"Tsu! Can you open the door?"

There was silence.

"Tsu, do you copy? You should be able to open the door. Try it right now!"

There was more silence. With fear beginning to turn to sadness, Chris went back to the switchboard. He looked all around it, searching for another switch that might work. But none of it made sense. He was about to give up and run to the room, hoping he might somehow be able to force the door open. But too much time had already passed.

Then, the receiver crackled.

"Chris," Tsu's voice came faintly down the line.

"Tsu! What's happening? Are you okay?"

"We're out. Everybody's out."

Chris felt a surge of joy in his chest.

"Is anyone hurt?" he asked as he walked quickly towards the room.

"We all need help," Tsu said, "but medics are arriving."

Now back in the main part of the hotel, Chris saw that there were special forces everywhere. Osman's men were nowhere to be seen.

"You should be safe now," he told Tsu. "I'm going after McGoldrick."

Believing McGoldrick would be trying to make a quick escape, Chris made his way out of the building.

Outside, it was frantic. Among the police, ambulances, and huddled groups of terrified hotel guests, Chris could see that special forces had killed or rounded up the shooters. He now assessed that the role of the shooters must have been to create a diversion, to keep security personnel occupied while the targets were all quietly disposed of in one room.

He looked across the grounds and could see that McGoldrick's motorcade was still on the property and stationary. He moved away from the main entrance to do a perimeter check.

Through manicured gardens, he entered an area of strange tranquility. There were no people in the gardens, but the fountains trickled on, and the birds had already forgotten the sound of gunshots and returned to the trees.

Then, Chris was brought back to the brutality of the situation. Through the trees, he could hear angry shouting. He stepped up his pace and moved in the direction of the noise.

He made his way through the greenery, and emerged on the other side to see a strange sight. Next to a colorful flower bed, he saw McGoldrick on his knees, a look of desperation on his face. Standing over him was a stocky man dressed in black, holding a gun to McGoldrick's forehead. The guy was wearing a flak jacket and a bullet belt. He looked like a member of McGoldrick's own security personnel rather than Osman's.

"There were children in there, you ass!" the man yelled at McGoldrick, his voice shaking with anger.

"Sir," Chris said, loudly enough to get the man's attention but not startle him into doing anything he would regret. The man's head spun around, but his gun remained on McGoldrick.

"Sir, I know you're angry. But this is not the right option," Chris told him.

"He tried to kill children with gas!" the man shouted. "He's an animal and he deserves to die."

"But you don't deserve to spend the rest of your life locked up. He will be punished, but not like this."

The guy looked back at McGoldrick, his mind conflicted.

"Are you a ex-military, sir?" Chris asked, knowing a lot of guys with D.C. security firms were ex-service.

"Yes, sir."

"Then I would ask you to remember your training and stay calm. You can do a lot of good for the world, but not from behind bars. I also have every reason to hate this man, but this is not the way to end this."

"I know who you are, sir."

"Then you'll know what I was accused of. And McGoldrick framed me for it. You can now testify what kind of person he is."

"I've suspected him for a long time, but I didn't wanna lose my job. But today I put a listening device on him and I heard him tellin' someone: 'release the gas.'"

"That's good work. Now, let's finish the job properly. Get him face down on the ground then call in your team."

The man hesitated for a second, then forced McGoldrick's face hard into the ground and pinned it down with his boot. Chris took only a brief glimpse at McGoldrick's pathetic face.

"What's your name, sir?" Chris asked.

"Harrison. Jim Harrison."

"Jim, I need you to do something for me. It's important. I need you to ask the most senior person in your detail to contact the authorities in D.C., tell them about McGoldrick, and also tell them that Helen Miller, the Director of the CIA, is working with him. Coming from you, someone should finally believe it."

Harrison looked stunned at the revelation, but quickly radioed in with the information.

Standing in the quiet hotel grounds, Chris reflected that if at any point during the last few weeks he had found himself with a gun to McGoldrick's head, it might have been him that had to be talked down.

Then, Harrison's radio crackled. Chris could hear the message that came back down the line: "Helen Miller is on the run. Repeat: Helen Miller has absconded."

"Miller is on the run, sir," Harrison informed Chris.

"Thanks, I heard it. Now it's her turn to find out how tough being on the run really is."

Members of Harrison's team then arrived, cuffed McGoldrick, and dragged him up roughly off the ground.

"Make sure he gets back to the States in one piece," Chris said to the lead. "It's important I get to interrogate him."

The lead guy nodded at Chris, then said:

"If you need a ride home, be at the helipad in twenty minutes."

"Thank you, sir," Chris replied. Then, he turned and went to find Tsu.

Outside the room they had been trapped in, he found the ambassador, his family, and several others sitting on the ground being attended to by medical professionals.

He couldn't see Tsu. He then spun around and saw that she was on her feet, helping to tend to the injured.

"Are you okay?" Chris asked, putting his hand gently on her arm as he looked into her eyes. "You need to be getting attention too."

"I'm fine," she said, smiling.

"That's so great to hear. Can I talk to you?" he asked.

"Sure."

He led her to the far end of the corridor where they could talk in private.

"I don't know how the Moroccan authorities are going to treat me at this point," he explained. "What they know or what they don't. I have the opportunity to return to the States right now, and I need to take it."

Tsu nodded, looking at him intently as he continued:

"I have no idea what your next move might be, but if you wanted to come back…"

Tsu was suddenly wide-eyed and terrified, a look that made Chris stop what he was saying. Then, he noticed she was looking over his shoulder.

He turned around to see Osman standing behind him. His left eye was totally gone, and the left side of his face a gory mess. But he was on his feet. And he was holding a gun.

"Not a damn sound," he growled. Chris and Tsu raised their hands.

"Which one of you wants to die first?" Osman asked, quiet but menacing.

Chris put himself between Tsu and Osman, then said:

"Let us go, and I'll do everything in my power to make sure you're treated fairly when the shit comes down."

"Fucking hero," Osman replied. "I'll be dead before then. Get on your knees."

"Look," Chris said. "We can…"

"Get on your knees!" Osman yelled.

Tsu and Chris began to sink slowly to their knees, both of them trying desperately to think of a way to talk Osman down. But they only had a few seconds left.

"You can go first, bitch," Osman told Tsu, pointing the gun past Chris and towards her forehead. "They'll have to clean that pretty face off the wa—"

From behind Osman, a golf club came swinging through the air. It smashed into his cheek with such force that his head seemed to bend in two. As he fell, Chris and Tsu saw the man standing behind him. The man who had saved their lives.

"And that was only a practice swing," Ned said, before slinging the club to the ground.

Chris looked at him in amazement.

"What the hell are you doing here?!" he asked.

"I think the question you meant to ask was: *how can I ever repay you for saving my life?*"

"Thank you, Ned!" Tsu said. "I mean, you're late, but."

"I wasn't even in Morocco when you called me! Coming to someone's rescue while you're on the run is not easy."

"I'll get the explanations later," Chris said, shaking his head. "Let's get out of here."

∼

"So just to be clear," Chris asked, "the person you spoke Korean to on the phone from the jail was *Ned?*"

"Yes," Tsu confirmed. "I had seen a brochure for the golf resort in Osman's room, and it was the only lead we had left. I asked Ned if he could get someone in the area to help us. As it turned out, the person he sent to help us was himself."

Smiling at Chris, she picked up a crystal tumbler filled with Scotch. They were in a luxe compartment of the private plane that had taken McGoldrick to Morocco. Now, he was in cuffs, and they were enjoying his whiskey supply.

"What is it that you're so surprised about?" Ned asked. "That I saved your lives or that I can speak Korean?"

"Both!" Chris said. "I mean, you've saved my skin many times from an office, but never on the ground. And I have certainly never heard you speak Korean."

"I like to keep a little mystery about me, even among old friends," Ned said.

Chris smirked as he took a sip.

"Speaking of mystery," he said, turning to Tsu. "I have great respect and admiration for you, Tsu. We have now been on two adventures together and I consider you a friend. But I just have one simple question: Who the hell are you?!"

"Great question," Ned said.

"Well, I promised I would tell you a little more about myself," Tsu told Chris, while looking to make sure the compartment door was closed. "So here goes. I was born in Japan. My mother was Japanese and my father was Korean. I moved to South Korea when I was young, and when I grew up I joined the National Intelligence Service. It was great for a while, but things went wrong. That's a story for another day. But long story short, the agency had a lot of factions. I ended up being run by one superior, off book. I had one person to report to, and one partner on the ground. That was all."

"Wow," Chris said. "Wait, you said you *had* one partner, does that mean you don't anymore?"

"He was killed in Yangon. He was arrogant and cavalier, and he probably got himself killed by giving himself away to the people he was supposed to be pursuing. Now, it's just me and my superior."

"I can tell you, I learned something new there too," Ned told Chris. "She has always kept me guessing also."

"Well, that does have to be my next question," Chris said. "How do you two know each other?"

"Ned made sure I was taken care of when a CIA agent left me in the lurch," Tsu explained. "I did a favor for him in return. Then I did many more, just because phone calls to him were pretty much the only enjoyable part of my work."

"I get a lot of people to do what I want because they

owe the CIA something," Ned said. "But some of them actually like me."

"I definitely like you," Tsu said, giving Ned a charming smile.

"I definitely like you, too," Chris joined in, knowing all this adoration would be too much for Ned to handle.

"Cool, you can all shut up now," Ned said. If he wasn't so red already, he might even have been blushing.

41

TURQUOISE WATER

I t was a cold, hard January in Washington D.C. when Chris walked through the tall gates of the McVey Correctional Center, the guard nodding at him as Chris showed his CIA ID.

He was led to a bare cell, where he watched as McGoldrick was brought to him by guards, his hands cuffed and his appearance wretchedly disheveled.

"I'm not going to tell you a thing," McGoldrick said, failing to look Chris in the eye as they both took a seat.

"I know you already spilled to the FBI, so you can drop the tough guy act," Chris said. "I just need a few answers of my own, and maybe we can get a little more off your sentence."

McGoldrick looked as if he might be about to cry.

"You told the FBI the plan for Rabat was for you to look like a hero. A hero who valiantly tried to stop terrorists, which would virtually guarantee you success in the election. But there's more to it than that. Much more."

McGoldrick briefly glanced at Chris's face, then looked away again.

"You, Miller, Osman, Lellouche. It's all connected. This is international, and it's widespread. Who's running it?"

McGoldrick just stared at the ground.

"I've been in this game a long time," Chris said. "Some people talk, and some don't. I know the ones who will talk, and you're one of them. Just get it all out now, and there's nothing left to lose. You can do your time and maybe one day start over."

McGoldrick sighed, then finally spoke.

"Like you said, there is a lot going on with this shit. I don't know all of it. But there is one guy running everything from the top. At some time in his past, someone in D.C. really screwed him over. It started out as revenge, but God knows what it has spiraled into now."

"Keep talking."

"I don't have a name. That's the truth. But I know there's a connection to a secret society. Maybe the Skull and Bones."

"Yale."

"Yeah. And I know he recruits people who are compromised. He gets them with blackmail."

"Is that how he got you?"

McGoldrick sighed again, heavier.

"Yes. I already told everything to the FBI. It was in my past."

"What about Helen? How did he get her?"

"Honduras. Someone there really hurt her bad. A few years later, she went back off-book to take him out. Didn't know his kids were there, and ended up taking them out too."

Chris felt his stomach tighten. He didn't let on to McGoldrick that he had been with Helen in Honduras the first time around. He knew the ordeal had messed her up, but he had no idea how badly.

"Is there anything else you can tell me? Anything at all?"

"There is one more thing. The guy running the show is one ugly bastard. I caught a glimpse of him once. Big jowls, pitted skin. I would say he looks like a bulldog but that's unfair on those creatures."

The interview was interrupted by a guard.

"Sir, it's time for the prisoner to attend his court appearance," the guard told Chris. "The interview will have to end there."

Chris stood and McGoldrick was led out of the cell.

Outside the prison walls, Chris waited in his car for the vehicle that was transporting McGoldrick to emerge. He planned to attend the court appearance to see if he could learn anything more from what McGoldrick said during the hearing.

The vehicle carrying McGoldrick exited the prison grounds, and Chris dropped behind to follow the convoy that was escorting the high-profile prisoner.

Thirty minutes later, he had ditched his car and was trying to make his way on foot through the crowds surrounding the courthouse, a mixture of people who were outraged, fascinated, or both.

McGoldrick's head was covered with a towel as he was taken toward the courthouse. But he never made it through the door. A bullet, from somewhere up high, pierced his skull. Chris watched as his body collapsed to the floor.

In the hysteria that followed, Chris saw one thing that stood out clear as day. Among the running people gripped by mass panic, Chris saw a young man with French-cropped blond hair walking calmly away, wearing an earpiece and trying to hide a satisfied smile on his face. It was a face that Chris recognized. He had seen it several months before, standing on the deck of a boat that had smashed into his own.

A WEEK after the shooting at the courthouse, Chris was on the deck of a boat off the coast of Florida Keys. He took out his phone and dialed, not knowing whether the person he was calling would answer.

The phone rang for a long time, and he was about to cut the call when Tsu finally answered.

"Yes?"

"Tsu, it's Chris."

"Oh! Thank God. Most of the people who call me, I do not like."

"I know the feeling. I just wanted to check in, see how you're doing?"

"Thank you. Not so great though … I just heard my superior has been killed. Must have been only a short time after I last spoke to him when I was in Bamako."

"I'm very sorry to hear that. Were you close?"

"To be honest, not really. But it's still so sad. And it leaves a void, you know? I feel kind of lost."

Chris paused briefly, then said:

"Well, I'm on a boat sailing the Florida Keys right now. I need to do some thinking, and when I need to think, I sail."

"Florida Keys sounds wonderful," Tsu replied.

"Yeah. There are worse places to be lost, so if you feel like hopping on a plane down to Florida, I'd be glad to fix you a Scotch. We could do some sailing and thinking together."

"As it happens, I drink Scotch when I need to think, so that sounds just perfect."

Chris looked out at the beautiful turquoise water, and allowed himself a moment of happiness.

"Wonderful. See you soon," he said.

THE END

CHRIS COLLINS RETURNS IN SHANGHAI CROSSFIRE!

GET IT NOW!

TURN THE PAGE FOR AN EXCERPT FROM THE EXPLOSIVE NEW NOVEL BY JOHN HOPTON AND DAVID BERENS.

SHANGHAI CROSSFIRE

A CHRIS COLLINS CIA THRILLER #2

1

MOONLIGHT AND WHISKEY

Chris Collins was used to playing it cool. As a trained spy and a man who had experienced plenty, he could keep his emotions in check and his feelings hidden. That's why he was surprised when he felt his stomach turn to mush and his heart flutter at the sight of a woman. It was like the years had been stripped away and he was fifteen again.

This was a woman he had laid eyes on many times before. But as she stepped out of the Caribbean Sea, droplets of water glistening on her lightly tanned skin, feelings he had been trying to suppress came racing to the surface.

"Shall we get a drink?" Tsu asked as she approached his hammock. She swayed gently as she shook seawater from her long black hair that matched the color of her bikini.

"Oh, do you drink?" Chris asked. Tsu smiled.

"Occasionally," she replied.

They had now been in the Caribbean for two weeks, and had probably drunk more than most people drink in a year.

Just good ol' drinking buddies, Chris thought to himself. He smirked slightly as he climbed down from his hammock, his feet landing in soft white sand.

"What?" Tsu asked, raising an eyebrow at his smile.

"I was just thinking we should get a new hobby. Or at least mix things up a little."

"What did you have in mind?"

"I dunno. Fishing?"

"Sounds great. Rod in one hand, cocktail in the other."

Chris even found Tsu's enthusiasm for drinking endearing, despite it being partly responsible for his many recent hangovers. He resisted the urge to glance across and remind himself what great shape she was in ... in spite of her love of booze.

"Or surfing?" he suggested.

"Looks pretty difficult to hold a cocktail on one of those things," Tsu replied, gazing out over the beach to where a guy was riding the waves just off shore.

"Okay, forget it!" Chris said, quickly giving up the idea of giving up drinking. They trudged up to the ramshackle beach bar where they had spent every sunset for the past week, and found the bartender already grinning and waving a cocktail shaker at them.

"Do we have any money?" Tsu asked as they sat on long stools planted in the sand.

"Later, later," the bartender said, interrupting Chris

as he was about to answer in the negative. They hadn't been charged a dime since the first night.

"Thanks, Sam," Chris told the bartender.

"Thanks ... again!" Tsu said.

"If we don't need to pay, why not go ahead and get one for yourself, Sam?" Chris added. "On us."

"Thanks," the bartender replied. "But I'll leave you two alone to gaze into each other's eyes."

Chris and Tsu frowned at one other like it was the weirdest comment they had ever heard.

"Who should we drink to?" Tsu asked as Sam walked off down the beach, his waist-length dreadlocks swinging behind him.

"Ned?" Chris replied, thinking of his friend. Ned was a CIA analyst who had helped Chris out of many scrapes during his career.

"Sure, we haven't drunk to him for at least twenty-four hours," Tsu said, then added: "Shouldn't we try calling him again soon?"

They clinked glasses and took a sip of sensationally refreshing Guaro Sour.

"I really think it's useless," Chris replied. "He told me he wants to be left alone to concentrate on his sulking. And his drinking."

Late afternoon heat was radiating up from the sand as shadows lengthened, and surfers came in from the sea to shower and enjoy the balmy evening.

"Well, he could drink with us, we're only a flight away."

"He's feeling sorry for himself. And I can't say I blame

him. He lost his job, has no income ... and it's probably my fault."

"How many times does he have to tell you it's not your fault?" Tsu asked, reaching over the bar to grab a bottle of rum. She noticed the surprise on Chris's face.

"Sam told me it was fine to help myself," she explained, smiling.

"I have no idea how that guy makes a living," Chris replied. "Anyway, back to Ned. Whatever anyone says, he was secretly helping me with CIA resources when I was on the run. That must've played a part in him getting fired."

"If they were going to fire him for that, they would have fired him as soon as they found out. But the day they actually fired him was the day he put whiskey in his pot of curry noodles at lunchtime, then asked the new Director what the dirty videos in his search history had to do with national security."

"That would be enough to get someone fired," Chris admitted. "Everyone knows the old guy's reputation, but they usually don't say it to his face." Tsu glugged some neat rum into his empty glass, the red rays of the setting sun glistening on the surface of the liquid.

"How about we find somewhere for dinner?" she asked.

"I think we know what our dinner options are."

"Option."

"Exactly."

For the past week, they had been staying at the Lazy Lizard surf hostel, living like twenty-something backpackers only with less money. Chris had intended to sail around the Caribbean for a week or so to clear his head after a crazy few months. A few months during which he'd had to flee to Europe to clear his name after a heinous false accusation, uncovering a dangerous global conspiracy in the process—with Tsu's help.

Then Tsu had joined him in the Caribbean, and they were soon having far too much of a good time to force themselves to go home. The only person who had kept Tsu loosely tied to her country's intelligence service had been killed, and the tie had been cut completely. She was now very highly trained but very unemployed.

Chris had been reinstated at the CIA, but it didn't take much sailing and head-clearing before he realized his heart was no longer in it. He knew he had to investigate what the hell was going on with the conspiracy that had sucked in his former boss, Helen Miller—the ex-CIA Director—and Senator McGoldrick. But it was hard to do that under the direction of the CIA when he found it difficult to trust a single soul who still worked there.

He knew the majority were still good people, but after everything he had been through, he couldn't help but suspect everyone. And after the compensation claim that had crushed him financially, and with divorce imminent, he was broke.

Regardless of either Tsu or Chris's predicaments, they had sailed up to Emerald Bay, Jamaica, with a few dollars in their pockets and stayed much longer than they intended. Even if they did have money, there were no banks nearby. There was nothing but sea, sand, surfers … and, of course, booze.

"So, it's the fish restaurant again?" Tsu asked. Chris smiled at the use of the word "restaurant", knowing she was referring to their only dinner option: to sit around a fire with the backpackers and wait for the local fishermen to bring over the catch of the day, which they sold dirt cheap. Then the loud, bearded kid from Sydney, Australia, would insist on cooking the fish on the fire. Tsu and Chris had grown tired of arguing with him and trying to persuade him that he overrated his own cooking skills.

"I think I'll go for the monkfish burned beyond recognition tonight," Chris said, downing another rum. "Should we dress for dinner?"

"I like the casual look," Tsu said.

Chris watched as her eyes traced the lines of his shoulders. He followed her gaze down past the buttons of his light blue shirt to his exposed thighs and calf muscles dusted with sand. He almost said something about her indulgent eyeful, but left it alone.

"And people used to say I was a sharp dresser," Chris said. "I think I have been wearing this shirt for six days straight."

They stood from the bar and walked down to the sea, then strolled along the shore to where a fire was being lit.

"I can live without refined food," Chris said, "but I do miss Glenfiddich."

"Definitely," Tsu agreed. "If I ever get another pay packet, I'm going to buy the best Scotch I can find."

They reached the fire, where a group of backpackers had gathered for a night of drinking and bullshitting. A guy with a ponytail was pouring out brown booze from an unmarked bottle.

"Heyyy!" he said when he spotted Chris and Tsu. He handed them drinks, touched plastic cups, and stumbled.

Plenty of rough booze duly flowed, and was followed by an inadequate meal of burned-black fish. Everyone was sitting cross-legged in the sand after dinner when the Aussie kid posed a question to the group.

"Hey, anybody here ever been in a fight?" he asked. Everybody was silent, knowing the question was simply a lead into his own anecdote.

"I was, once," he continued. "It was crazy. Some guy cut me up at the lights, then gave me the finger. He obviously didn't know I was a wrestler in high school. I was outta the car and hammerin' on his window before he knew what was happenin'. He tried to play the tough guy, opened his window and started givin' me shit. So I grabbed ahold a' his collar and tried to drag him right outta the car. Then the cops showed up. It was crazy."

There was a moment of silence.

"That's not a fight, dude," a French guy said calmly from across the fire, then went back to his book. Chris noted that the French guy had been there every night but always said very little.

"What? Yeah, it is...," the Aussie kid said, looking crestfallen. "Okay, who has a better story, then?"

More silence. Then the kid noticed that Chris was smiling at the French guy's response.

"How about you, Chris? You ever been in a fight?" he asked.

"I got in a fight in high school," Chris replied. "Pretty sure I lost."

It was true he had been in a fight in high school. He just didn't mention the many he'd been in since … often against a foe with a knife or a gun.

"I've killed fourteen people," Tsu suddenly announced. After a brief pause, everyone laughed out loud.

"Let's take a stroll," Chris whispered in her ear. They stood and left the group as somebody was picking up a guitar.

"What? They think it's a joke!" Tsu said.

"I know, it was funny," Chris replied. "It's just that I couldn't take anymore of that guy's ridiculous stories."

Tsu laughed.

"How about we chill on the boat?" she asked. "The drinks cabinet has been empty for days, though."

"We could just enjoy the moonlight?" Chris suggested.

"I do love moonlight. But moonlight and whiskey, now that's a combination."

Chris smiled and shook his head.

"Okay, we'll make a stop at Sam's."

Twenty minutes later, they were lying on their backs on the deck of their cabin cruiser, sipping whiskey and gazing up at the stars.

"I really can't face going back to D.C.," Chris said.

"But you need to save the world, right?" Tsu told him,

the corners of her mouth raising into a smile in the dark.

"Oh, yeah. I forgot about that."

"But seriously," Tsu continued. "This nasty piece of work that's running everything, whoever he is, needs to be stopped. Wiping out good people so he can put his own in power, and not caring who's killed in the crossfire. These people even tried to have you imprisoned and killed to keep you out of their way. It's insane."

"It sure is. I've been thinking it over, and there are two leads: the blond kid and Helen. And nobody knows where Helen is."

"So we go after the blond kid," Tsu said.

"We?" Chris asked. "Can I count on your help?"

"Sure you can. I mean, I have nowhere else to go."

"Well, if you're all out of options…"

Smiling more broadly, Tsu turned to look at Chris, then back up at the stars.

Staring into the cloudless Caribbean sky, Chris felt the gentlest touch on his hand, then Tsu's fingers slipped between his. He waited a moment before he turned to look at her. When he did, she held his gaze, her eyes having softened like he had never seen before. Chris ran his hand slowly up her back as their faces moved closer, and he could smell the salt on her skin.

Their lips touched softly, and they sank into a kiss with a mixture of desire and relief. It was like something had been completed. Tsu brushed her hand across Chris's cheek, then let her fingers slide into the hair at the back of his head as the kiss grew more intense. They were both without thoughts.

Wood snapped and splintered as bullets tore into the boat, ripping Chris and Tsu from their perfect moment and slamming them back into the real world. Chris covered Tsu's head as they quickly pulled themselves together and moved on their bellies across the deck. The bullets came thick and fast with a noise that was always terrifying even to people who had been in situations like this before. Chris and Tsu had been in plenty, but they had never been less prepared for it.

"Where's the shooter?" Tsu hissed.

"Must be on the beach," Chris replied. "There are no weapons on the boat. If we can't fight back, we have to run."

He signaled for Tsu to follow him towards the wheel, then ran in a crouch across the deck. The gunfire suddenly stopped, and the two of them were left with the sound of their own heavy breathing.

"Are you okay?" Chris asked, looking Tsu over for any sign of injury.

"I think so."

Chris turned to the ignition switch and tried to start the boat. The engine spluttered, then failed. He tried again, but this time it didn't make a sound.

"Shit," he growled, looking around to see what damage had been done. But another quick round of bullets came raining in, destroying the glass around the helm and sending them crashing back to the deck.

Crouching in the semi-darkness, Tsu's head swiveled around, scanning the area she could reach without leaving cover. Chris pointed to a rusty scaling knife tucked into a leather sheath under the steering column.

"How's your aim?" Tsu asked.

"Decent, but we only have one of those things."

"I used to practice every day when I was a kid," Tsu said. "I used to throw until I could stick a knife in a doll's eye from thirty meters.

"Girls will be girls," Chris said, managing sarcasm. "But had you downed nine or ten rums when you did it?"

"No," Tsu replied, picking up the knife. "But there's nothing like being shot at to sober you up."

They moved back into the open, leopard crawling across the deck and peering towards the beach.

"There," Chris whispered, gesturing towards an overturned rowing boat on the beach. Behind it, there seemed to be a mop of messy black hair shimmering in the moonlight.

"Maybe fifteen meters?" Tsu asked.

Chris nodded. Keeping low, Tsu crouched on her toes, tensing to spring up when the gunman raised his head to fire.

"Go for the shoulder," Chris said. "More chance of hitting, and we need him alive."

Chris watched as Tsu narrowed her eyes, training them on the man she was trying to neutralize. The section of beach was empty and the night was quiet. The rhythmic lapping of waves against the hull was oddly calming.

The man lifted his head slightly, and Tsu didn't waste a second. Before he'd even raised himself enough to shoot, she drew back her arm and flung it forward, releasing the knife straight and true. Chris braced for the sound of bullets, but all that came was a wail of shock and pain as the knife plunged into the attacker. Tsu grinned with pride at her score.

Chris leapt over the side of the boat and slushed through the waves towards the shore. Tsu quickly followed him into the water.

Chris emerged onto the beach as the attacker was trying to get to his knees. Before the guy could stand, Chris ripped the rifle from his hands and swung the heavy end in an arc through the air, hammering it into his jaw. The man slumped onto the sand as Tsu ran up.

The guy was skinny and frail. He wore tattered clothes, not fatigues or military gear. Now in the fetal position, possibly unconscious, and with blood pouring from his head, he looked pitiful. Nothing like a trained killer.

Chris crouched down to check he hadn't killed the man with one blow. But as he reached out to check for a pulse, the man whisked something out of his pocket. Chris felt a searing pain in his eyes. He covered his face, but it was too late. Pepper spray had rendered him blind.

Chris heard Tsu cry out:

"Motherfucker!"

Instinctively, Chris stumbled back away from the man on the ground. He knew the guy was badly injured, but he also knew that He and Tsu were now incapacitated.

"We need to wash our eyes!" Tsu yelled, breathing hard.

"Salt water will sting like hell," Chris said, "but hell is all we've got."

Chris felt a hand on his shoulder and braced himself to fight blind.

"Dude, don't hit me. It's me, Sam. You okay, man?

"This shit messed me up worse than your booze," Chris said, trying to open his eyes to look at Sam. It was too painful.

"Piece of shit pepper sprayed ya," Sam said.

"We know!" Tsu shouted.

"I've seen worse," Sam informed them as he wiped the burning chemical away with a wet cloth.

"His aim wasn't the best," Chris said. "We probably got off easy. Still stings like hell though."

"Where is he, Sam?" Tsu asked. "Make sure he doesn't run."

"Too late," Sam said. "He moved off into the trees when he saw me coming." He pointed towards the edge of the rainforest at the back of the beach, even though nobody could see him pointing.

"Then that's where we're going," Chris said.

"Not until you get your eyes back," Sam replied.

"It will take at least fifteen minutes to get our sight back," Chris said. "And it's dark anyway."

"He won't get far," Tsu said. "He got a knife in the shoulder and a blow to the head. He's probably on his hands and knees."

"Sit on the beach and don't move," Sam instructed. "I'll be back with the maggot soon."

Still unable to see, Chris pictured Sam as he strode

towards the jungle, his long hair swaying behind.

"We really owe that guy," Chris said. "I mean, 'thanks' just ain't gonna cut it."

"I know," Tsu said. "So, you ever been pepper sprayed before?"

"Once, during my training. We had to learn what to expect. But I think they went easy on us back then. This is *goddamn* painful."

Tsu started to laugh.

"What?!" Chris asked.

"I dunno, this is weird! I can hear you but I can't see you. And I'm in terrible pain but I'm laughing."

"This *is* weird," Chris agreed. He then realized his sight was slowly returning. "Hey, can you see yet?"

"No!" Tsu replied.

Chris turned his head towards the jungle, and through bleary eyes he saw a shape coming out of the trees.

"That's a shame," he said. "Because you're missing a scene."

Sam was returning with the body of a scrawny man slung over his shoulder like a roll of carpet.

"Wait! I *can* see," Tsu said, just as Sam approached and dumped the man onto the beach, his breath blasting out of him as he landed hard on his back.

"What you wanna do with this piece of scum?" Sam asked.

"You got any rope?" Chris said.

"Sure."

. . .

IN THE DEAD OF NIGHT, at the back of the beach shack where Tsu and Chris had spent so many serene hours, the three of them stood around a trembling man who was sitting in the mud, tied to a pole.

"Who are you?" Chris asked. The man didn't reply. Sam sighed and took one step towards him.

"Okay, okay!" the guy blurted out in a thick Mexican accent. "I didn't wanna do it. They made me."

"Who made you?" Chris said.

"Please, I can't." The man looked like he was about to sob.

"You don't have to worry about what they'll do to you," Tsu told him. "Because whatever you tell us, I'm gonna cut your throat very soon. But if you cooperate, I'll make it quick."

The sobbing quickly arrived.

"Your name, and the name of your handler," Chris said.

"My name don't matter. I'm nobody. I just made a big mistake. Now I pay for it."

Chris already knew where this was going. The network he had uncovered recruited people with skeletons in their closet that they didn't want to let out. Someone promised to keep their secret if they just did a few little favors, but there were never enough favors, and each one was more awful than the last.

"Who's running you?" Tsu asked.

"I don't know his real name. Everybody calls him The Priest."

"What *do* you know about him?" Tsu said.

"I know getting involved with him is the stupidest thing I did in my life."

"Why?"

"The Priest … he does things to people. Things you wouldn't believe."

"Details," Chris said coldly. "The Priest is not who you need to be afraid of right now."

The man looked up at Chris. Hope was gone from his eyes.

"What's your name?" Chris asked.

"Miguel."

"And how do you know The Priest?"

"Drugs. I needed money. That was the only way to get it. He runs things in San Pablo."

"So I'm gonna take a guess. You started off dealing for a bit of money, but he quickly sucked you in. Soon, you had to do anything he asked."

"Right. Before I knew it, I was killing."

"And today, you were sent to kill me. And whoever might be with me."

"Yes."

"But we're not involved in drugs. Or Mexican gangs. Why?" Tsu asked.

"I don't know. They don't tell me. I'm sorr …" Miguel burst into tears before he could finish his sentence.

"It doesn't matter," Chris said. "I already know why, and I know who. The Priest is working for the same person that McGoldrick and Miller were. I don't know the bastard's name yet, but I'm going to find out."

CAGED RAT

I n a down-on-its-luck town in Bernalillo County, New Mexico, a boy's mother was talking about him in his absence. In fact, a lot of people talked about him in his absence, because he hadn't left his bedroom for two years.

"His demons are inside and out," his mother told her neighbor, who had visited for a quick chat five hours ago. "He always had it tough, you know that. He doesn't know how to talk to people—barely said a word in his life."

"I do know that. I remember," the neighbor confirmed.

"He didn't have a chance at happiness when it came time to go to school. And those bastards made damn sure he never got it."

"Those bastards."

"Not only those evil little kids. The damn teachers too. Treated him like his problems were plain stubbornness. Like not talkin' was just bein' lazy. I told 'em, 'he don't even tell me when he's sick.' They didn't give a shit."

Two years earlier, when he was fourteen years old, Sheldon Norris stopped going to school. He came home one day and went right up to his room, just like he did every night. Only this time, he didn't come out. When his mom asked him to come down for dinner, he just shook his head.

"What really gets my goat," the neighbor said, "is that he is one of the kindest, smartest kids I ever met. Least, he was when I ever met him. For all I know, they beat it outta him."

"He is still smart, I can tell you that," Sheldon's mom, Jean, said. Some of the crazy shit I see on his computer screen, I have no idea what it is, but he's doin' somethin' up there."

"Bad somethin' or good somethin'?"

"I can't say for sure. But it's somethin'. Maybe math, science. I dunno. He don't seem to care if I spot it, coz he knows I can't understand it."

Up in his room, Sheldon was hurting. His eyes were hurting from staring at the screen in 24-hour darkness, because he refused to open the blinds. His stomach was hurting because it was always empty. Most days, he just couldn't make himself eat. He was in emotional pain too, feeling like his heart was breaking.

It was five in the afternoon, and he knew his mom would soon be up to ask him to eat something. He told himself he was going to smile at her today.

He had to let her know that he didn't blame her for anything, that he was sorry for letting her down, and he was grateful that she continued to take care of him even though he gave nothing back.

Every day, he told himself he would smile. But the last one he'd managed was a week ago. He closed down some of the dozens of windows he had open on his computer screen, eventually landing on a chat room.

"CagedRat365, you there?" someone asked him on the chat window. It was a user he was sick of talking to, who seemed to know nothing about the subject he was supposed to be on there to talk about.

"No," Sheldon typed. He closed the window.

Downstairs, the sun that Sheldon never saw streamed through the living room window as it slid down the sky.

"So, Lilly, is it 'bout time for somethin' a little stronger than coffee?" Jean asked her neighbor. "How about we go out on the porch and have a sundowner?"

"You say that every day like you had the idea for the first time!" Lilly replied, laughing as she stood. "And anyways, it's almost dark already."

"Well okay, we'll toast the moon."

"Let me use the bathroom while you make the drinks." Lilly said. "Then we'll toast that moon."

"Well, if you insist!" Jean said.

After using the bathroom, Lilly washed her hands. She smiled at herself in the mirror, then checked her hair.

As she reached for the door, she heard a bloodcurdling scream from the kitchen.

"Oh no, Jean, no, no!" she cried. She thought her friend must have had a terrible accident.

Her heart pounding, she ran to where Jean had gone to make the drinks. She froze in horror at what she saw.

Jean's body was on the ground, her eyes lifeless. Her throat was cut open. Standing over her was a man dressed completely in black, including the surgical mask covering his face.

Even his eyes seemed black, as he stared through Lilly like she wasn't there. But he acknowledged her presence long enough to step to her and open her throat too. Fear had paralyzed her, leaving her unable to defend herself.

After placing Lilly's body next to Jean's on the floor, the man in black made his way purposefully through the house. The old wooden stairs creaked as he climbed them, alerting Sheldon to somebody making their way up.

Sitting cross-legged in his room, Sheldon prepared to try to interact with his mother, but hoped she would go to a different room and save him the anguish of failing.

When the man opened the door and stepped silently into the room, Sheldon could not react. He had no way to deal with what he was seeing.

For a second, he wondered if this was someone from the authorities come to make him become part of society again. But the man's clothes, and more importantly the evil in his eyes, let him know it was much worse.

The man strode over to Sheldon, stepping over cables and scattered clothes, and towered over him, pausing for a brief moment. Then he grabbed Sheldon by the hair, took a small canister from his pocket, and sprayed the contents into the boy's face. Sheldon lost consciousness immediately.

3

THE PRIEST

This was probably the reddest Ned had ever been. Sitting under the sun in Baku, Azerbaijan, he sweated, drank, and sweated some more. He was used to sitting in a darkened office looking at data. He was not used to the strong sun of the Caucasus, and was even less able to cope with the 70 percent alcohol content in the Azerbaijani araf he had been drinking.

The agonized wail of a woman singing Azerbaijani folk music assaulted his ears, and he found himself squeezing his eyes closed as if that was somehow going to help. Finally, mercifully, the singing stopped.

"Time for the main event!" Ned's companion shouted, slapping Ned hard on the shoulder. Murad was very excited about the main event.

"What's the main event?" Ned asked, shielding his eyes as he turned to look at the man he had met just a few days earlier but who had quickly become his drinking buddy.

"Wrestling!" Murad replied.

Ned glanced across the crowded park they were sitting in. It was filled with men showing off immaculate gym bodies and women who all looked like supermodels. Tall trees partially obscured the even taller buildings of the glistening, newly rich city, and an occasional breeze drifted in from the Caspian Sea. In the middle of the park, a wrestling ring was being prepared for battle.

"Yes!" Murad exclaimed. "Lucy!"

Murad was looking toward an extremely large man with fat piled on muscle. The man was also very tall and very hairy, his hair and beard forming a circular mane around his head.

"That's ... Lucy?" Ned asked.

"Yes!" Murad confirmed. "He's number one wrestler in Baku!"

"I can see why," Ned said.

"When he was a baby, he drank buffalo milk!"

"What? ... Why?"

"To make strong!"

"I don't ... I don't see why that would make someone strong?" Ned enquired.

Murad ignored him.

"I mean, what's the science behin ..."

"Yaaaaaaaasssss!" Murad bellowed as Lucy approached the ring, drowning out Ned's cynicism. Murad was now on his feet, yelling and waving both fists in the air. The rest of the people in the park grew more animated too, and Ned suddenly felt excited to see the event. Then, his phone buzzed.

He looked at the screen and saw it was Chris. He briefly hesitated, then thought:

No, I can't ignore my good friend just to watch a man called Lucy slap another man for sport.

He put the phone to his ear and answered:

"I told you, I'm not coming back."

"I know. I just want to hear how you're doing. What are you up to?"

"Drinking, sulking, and watching wrestling."

"Like a teenager?"

"Yes."

"Where are you?"

"Baku."

"Of course," Chris said facetiously. "Listen, once again, I'm sorry about getting you fired."

"Buddy, I told you. It wasn't helping you that got me fired. It was telling the new Director to quit looking at smut during a time of national crisis. And maybe because I put whiskey in my curry noodles."

"That's good to know. But still, thanks for everything you did."

"Any time."

"Really? Great, because I have a tiny favor to ask."

"I thought you wanted to know how I was doin'?"

"I did. I wanted to check what's up and get a little intel on a Mexican drug lord. Standard call."

"You want to know about The Priest."

"Yes. I guess you talked to Tsu already."

"I sure did. And I'll tell you the same thing I told her: stay away,"

Ned's voice was drowned out by delighted cheers from the crowd as Lucy slammed some poor guy head first into the mat.

"Not that simple," Chris replied.

"I'm pretty sure it is. It's not The Priest you want. It's the guy at the top. The guy that was running McGoldrick, Miller, and is somehow connected to The Priest. But there are other routes."

"I'm trying all routes. I know he's connected to a drug cartel, that was easy to find out. What I need is detail."

Ned sighed.

"I worked on a case he was linked to. Years ago. There are three things you need to know about The Priest. One, he is extremely suave. Dresses immaculately, and people compliment him on his class even though they know the dark reality. Two, he is a gambler. It's a major addiction, but he has the money to feed it.

"And what's the third?"

"The third is he's an egomaniac. A narcissist. If anyone challenges him, even if it's only by dressing better, he despises it."

"I knew you were the right man to call," Chris said. "How about get the hell out of Baku and come back to help me?"

"If what you need help with is drinking and watching wrestling, I'm your guy," Ned replied, flapping his garish Hawaiian shirt to get air to his chest.

"Okay, I get it. Do what you need to do. When you've sobered up, give me a call. We'll get a drink."

"Roger that."

"And Ned, one more thing. Why is he called The Priest?"

"Good question. But that, my friend, I do not know. He has a lot of eccentricities. It could be a reference to any kind of creepy shit that we're yet to find out."

"Well, it sure is great to get back to the creepy shit," Chris said. "I'd had enough of cocktails and beaches anyway. Take it easy, buddy."

Two of the skills the CIA looks for when it's recruiting are an exceptional memory and incredible attention to detail. Chris had been raking through his memory looking for any detail that might help him.

He had very few leads to the man who had spent the last several months plotting to kill him ... and who seemed to have people all over the world who were willing to help. Helen Miller was missing and Matthew McGoldrick was dead after a shocking assassination outside a courthouse —almost certainly taken out before he could squeal.

That left the blond kid. The kid Chris had first seen standing shirtless on the deck of a boat that was far too expensive for a kid of his age to be in control of, jabbing his finger and sneering at Chris and Ned.

That was seconds after the kid's boat had smashed into Chris's. At the time, it had seemed like an accident resulting from extreme recklessness. In hindsight, it was clearly an attempt to damage Chris in someway. To disrupt his life, or possibly end it.

The following compensation claim had left Chris broke. The summons gave the name of a Mr. Blaine Havemeyer as the claimant, but Chris never had the chance to face the kid in court. His wife, already on the verge of leaving him, had begged Chris to settle out of court and put the incident behind them. She told Chris that Havemeyer's people were not the sort of people they should be dealing with. As it turned out, she was right.

She had been approached one night and threatened with terrible things if the case wasn't settled right away. Investigations into the man who had approached her, and even the name Blaine Havemeyer, had drawn blanks. Then, Chris had been falsely accused of a felony and gone on the run overseas, which it's fair to say put the investigation on the back-burner.

The second time he had seen the blond kid, it was outside the courthouse where Matthew McGoldrick had been assassinated. The kid was smirking, and Chris just knew he was somehow involved. The FBI agents tasked with investigating the assassination hadn't been too interested in the fact that Chris had seen a young man smiling outside a courthouse, which was understandable. Then again, their investigation had made little progress, so maybe they should have been focusing on the smaller details. Either way, Chris now wanted to tackle this alone. He didn't know who he could trust at the CIA, the FBI, or anywhere else.

Thinking back through the past months, one detail kept popping into his head. Standing next to the blond kid on the boat was a guy in a Yale University T-shirt. Anyone could wear a Yale University T-shirt, but there was more to it than that. These kids had *privileged frat boy* written all over them. It was highly likely they had gotten into some Ivy League college through connections rather than talent. And if you're at one Ivy League college, you don't go around wearing the logos of a rival one.

It was now clear that the blond kid's connection to McGoldrick wasn't only that he was there, smirking, when McGoldrick was assassinated. Shortly before he was killed, the senator had told Chris a detail about the group he was trying to investigate. Its leader had a connection to a secret society: The Skull and Bones. Yale.

It wasn't surprising that someone so powerful and influential would have connections to an elite secret society, in fact it would be expected. But the Yale shirt on the boat combined with the boss's own Yale connection gave Chris a place to start. And a name: Havemeyer. That's when he decided: he was going back to school.

4

BONESMEN

Beneath the imposing Gothic tower of the Sterling Memorial Library, Chris looked up towards the crisp blue sky over Yale University. He enjoyed a rare moment of peace before plunging into the rabbit warren of the library. Among the fifteen million books that make up the Yale University Library collection, Chris knew that one was named *The Order of the Skull and Bones*, a collection of rosters for members of the infamous Skull and Bones society.

The society was so secretive that during the past few decades, they had declined to reveal the names of their members at all. But membership to such prestigious societies often runs in families. Some or other Yale student deemed especially talented might be lucky enough to get a tap on the shoulder one day followed by an invitation to join. But the tap is far more likely to come if your name already fits.

Among the known names of the powerful alumni

were former U.S. presidents and presidential candidates, who were prepared to admit to their membership but not to disclose a single detail about what went on behind the closed doors of the society.

One president who had belonged to the Skull and Bones was William Howard Taft, whose father had founded the society in 1832. Chris also knew that several senior figures in the CIA were 'Bonesmen,' as the members called themselves.

But as a man who had risen to the top through hard work and talent rather than privilege, Chris hadn't rubbed shoulders with these people except on a purely professional basis. And besides, he no longer had enough faith in his CIA colleagues to ask any of them for insider information. His request could soon get back to the very people he was investigating.

Inside the magnificent building, which looked more like a cathedral than a library, Chris wanted to get a glimpse at the old rosters. He was hoping to find a link to Blaine Havemeyer, the name that had appeared on the summons during his compensation case. He made his way through the corridors of the library, past huge stone columns standing beneath a ceiling of ornately carved wood. He knew that he had two choices: spend hours looking for the right place, or ask a staff member to point to the exact location of the book he was searching for.

But his guard was raised so high that even mentioning the name of the book to the library staff might be revealing too much. So, he made a plan. He looked around for the most bored-looking student he could find.

He knew that a kid who wasn't even motivated enough to concentrate on the work that might land him a prestigious degree and a lucrative career definitely wouldn't care what random book some guy was looking for.

Fortunately, bored-looking students in a university library are not hard to come by. After a few minutes of searching, he found a kid who was slumped so far down into this seat he looked like he had melted. He was wearing earphones and staring straight ahead, his mouth slightly open. Chris walked up behind him and tapped him on the shoulder. Another student might have wondered if the tap was the beginning of a life-changing invitation to join the Skull and Bones society. But if this kid thought he was 'especially talented' then he was not only lazy but seriously deluded.

The kid jumped and spun his head around. Chris signaled for him to take out his earphones, then reached into his pocket and pulled out five crisp twenty dollar bills. Knowing he could submit it to the CIA as miscellaneous expenses, he was feeling extravagant. The kid frowned.

"Want to earn a quick buck?" Chris asked.

"Um. Okay."

"Tell the staff here you're looking for a book named *The Order of the Skull and Bones*. When they find it for you, bring it back to me but don't let the staff know it's for me. Simple."

Still frowning, the kid lurched towards the money.

"Not until I have the book," Chris said, pulling the notes out of reach.

"What's the book called?"

"I just told you."

"I forgot."

Feeling deeply concerned about the future of the country, Chris ripped a strip of paper off of the kid's notebook and wrote down the name of the book he was looking for.

"Okay," the kid said, taking the paper. He then shuffled off.

Ten minutes later, as Chris was leafing through a copy of Winston Churchill's *The Gathering Storm*, the kid shuffled back. He handed over the book with a vacant expression on his face. Chris stuffed the fifty bucks into his hand, then the kid turned and disappeared, saying nothing. Shaking his head in amazement that someone like that could make it into Yale, Chris crossed the library and found a quiet corner to hide away in.

He opened the book and ran his index finger down lists of names, a mix of well-known families and old-money surnames. Members' names had stopped being published before the time the society had supposedly opened up to start permitting women and taking in members from different cultural backgrounds.

As Chris was carefully scanning the alumni of 1927, his eyes widened as they landed on a name. A Hobert Myron Havemeyer. Chris noted the unusual nature of the given names. Also unusual was the fact that Havemeyer only appeared once, whereas other family names tended to run throughout. Then, he spotted something else. The given names, Hobert Myron, began to appear alongside a different surname: Landsdowne. Either there were two members with the same extremely unusual combination of given names, or the family name had been changed.

He thought it was entirely possible that some decades ago, Havemeyer had become Landsdowne. And the name Landsdowne was prevalent down the years. Could it be that the family he was pursuing had changed its name almost a century earlier but occasionally used the old name as a cover? He closed the book and left it on the desk before striding quickly out of the library.

Back in the bright winter sunlight, he walked to a quiet, leafy corner of campus and took out his phone. He felt a tinge of sadness as he dialed, because this was a situation in which he would previously have called Ned. Now, the phone call he made to CIA New Headquarters was answered by a young woman barely into her twenties.

"Lauren, I need a few things done urgently," Chris said when she answered.

"Okay."

"The first is to get any information you can on Yale alumni with the surname Landsdowne. They might be recent alumni or from many years ago, but they will be from money. In particular, look for information on a Blaine Landsdowne."

"Okay."

"The second thing is to find out anything you can about The Tomb; the meeting place of the Yale Skull and Bones society. What security measures they use; how often they meet. Anything you can."

"How do I do that?"

This time, Chris worried about the future of the CIA. He had no idea how Lauren had passed training.

"First, you search any published information," he told her. "Details from members who have spoken off-record to journalists. Look at information told to agents and logged. If you need to, get an agent into a rich kids' party. Even people who are sworn to secrecy like to brag."

"Don't we need special authorization to conduct operations against U.S. citizens?" Lauren asked.

Oh, that part of your training, you remember…, Chris thought.

"Don't worry about the authorization, Lauren. If the Director asks any questions, point him my way."

"Yes, sir."

"And you don't need to call me 'sir.'"

"Okay, Mister … officer …"

"Chris is fine."

"Okay. Bye."

5

FAR FROM GOOD

For the next few days, Chris hung around campus. He disguised himself with a fake gray beard, some tatty brown corduroy pants, and a tweed jacket with leather patches on the elbows. He completed the venerable university lecturer look by drooping his shoulders and dragging his feet when he walked, replacing his military posture with the one of someone who had spent years hunched over books.

As often as he could, he walked past The Tomb, the mysterious meeting place of the Skull and Bones. Given how unsure he was that Lauren would come through with good information, he had been reading up on the place himself. The windowless mausoleum built from brown sandstone had been the meeting place of the society since 1856. In the decades that followed, the roof eventually acquired a landing pad for private helicopters.

The Skull and Bones began as an occult society, and much of the decor and rituals that went on inside the building were inspired by those origins. Initiation is said to involve a coffin, and rooms adorned with black and red velvet have pentagrams on the walls.

Chris was taking his daily walk around campus, a leather satchel in one hand and a few books in the other, when he got a call from Lauren. He could just about make out her greeting through the sound of chewing. Clearly, she had chosen to eat lunch at the exact time she had called him.

"Lauren, what are you eating?" he asked.

"Oh," Lauren said. "It's just quinoa salad."

"I need you to listen to me very carefully. From now on I only want to see...or hear...you eating curry noodles for lunch, okay?"

"Um. Why do I ..."

"It's a direct order."

"But, I don't like ...,"

"It's okay, Lauren, you don't have to eat what I tell you. Enjoy your quinoa. What have you got for me?"

"So, I found out about The Tomb."

"Good."

"It is like a tomb with no windows."

"Okay,"

"It has a helipad on the roof,"

"Thanks, I knew that," Chris said, trying to be calm and polite while he was given information he was already aware of.

"And, there's likely to be a meeting this Friday night. We got someone talking to people on campus, and it sounds like they meet the last Friday of every month."

Chris was suddenly more enthusiastic about what Lauren could offer him.

"Great work, Lauren," he said. "What else?"

"I couldn't get any information on their security. It's extremely secretive. But I did get some information on Landsdowne. A Mr. Elias Faust Landsdowne, with Yale connections. And, he has a son named Blaine."

"Go on," Chris said.

"In the 1970s, Landsdowne was making a lot of money in Williamsburg County, South Carolina, running everything from banks to brothels. He pretty much ran a whole town, and he was starting to make moves in state politics. I found an image of his face on a billboard down there. I'm sending you some images now. He was one ugly guy.

"And I'm guessing he still is."

"Yeah. Anyway, just as things were going great for him, the Feds went down there and ruined everything. He'd been involved in fraud, corruption, even using illegal workers and paying them slave wages."

As Lauren spoke, Chris searched for images of Landsdowne. There were pictures of the man in his younger days, when he rubbed shoulders with notables before his reputation was ruined. Unsurprisingly, there were none from recent years. Chris zoomed in on a picture of Landsdowne's gnarled countenance. As he finally laid eyes on the man's face, he was filled with a mixture of hatred and red-hot anticipation at the thrill of the chase.

"He eventually got what was coming to him," Lauren

continued. "He did three years in Lieber Correctional Institution."

"Plenty of time to stew and wind himself up about how government stuck its nose in and spoiled his party," Chris said. "Plenty of time to plan his revenge, too. Lauren, you did a great job on this. I just need one more tiny thing. And I mean tiny."

FRIDAY NIGHT ROLLED AROUND, and Chris was in his lecturer gear walking campus grounds as the sun began to set. He stayed close enough to The Tomb to see anyone that might arrive and enter. Close to 8pm, people started showing up, and almost all of them were graying, middle-aged men wearing evening suits. But then, there was someone from a different generation. Someone of college age with a shock of blond hair.

Chris felt a surge of adrenaline. This was his chance. Adopting his elderly lecturer stoop, he made his way towards Blaine, who was striding towards The Tomb with a man of a similar age and the same confident gait. As the men chatted, Chris walked towards them looking like he was in a hurry. He stumbled as he approached, the books flying out of his arms. They landed at the men's feet.

"I'm so sorry," Chris said, holding his lower back as he bent down to pick up the books. The man with Havemeyer leaned down to help collect the books. Havemeyer, meanwhile, tutted at the pathetic old man in front of him, then turned away and took out his phone to pass the time while his friend offered assistance.

Down on the ground, Chris held a tiny listening device between his thumb and finger. Keeping his fingers away from the adhesive side, he quickly attached the bug to the fabric inside the man's suit, just above the ankle. Feigning difficulty, he stood.

"Thank you, sir," he said in a shaky voice as the man handed him the books. Then he walked away.

Sitting in his car a few blocks from campus, he got a flavor of how Skull and Bones meetings go down. After some ceremonial opening comments spoken partly in German, the evening was a mixture of political chat and off-color jokes, with an occasional comment about the quality of the wine thrown in. It was only after dinner that something truly strange happened.

A new member was introduced by a man whose voice Chris recognized as Havemeyer's. The member was invited to stand and speak. They delivered a full two hours of oral autobiography, including graphic accounts of sexual history and admissions of minor crimes. Chris realized it was all designed to give members information they could use if the member ever let the society down. It was insurance against betrayal. It provided an insight into the people he was dealing with, but it gave him nothing concrete. It was almost midnight when he got his lucky break.

"Let's go to a lounge," he heard Havemeyer say to someone. Chris hoped it was the man Havemeyer had arrived with. There was some shuffling followed by the closing of a door. Chris could hear two men talking, and knew the man he had bugged was still with Havemeyer. The next thing he heard was the tinkling of glasses and the gurgling of liquor being poured.

"Cognac Gautier," Havemeyer said. Our esteemed alumni have been drinking it since 1856. They just didn't know how great it is when paired with cocaine."

Havemeyer's sidekick laughed.

"Rack me up a line," Havemeyer instructed. Chris was grateful that his bug wasn't close to the man's nose, but he could still hear sickening snorts as the men vacuumed the powder up their nostrils. In a seemingly private room and with enough substances in their veins to loosen them up, they were in a talkative mood.

"While those old fuckwits talk dull D.C politics, we can talk real politics," Havemeyer said.

"How's the clean up going?" his sidekick asked between sniffs.

"Well, we blew McGoldrick's brains out, so I think we can say he's taken care of. Next on the list is Miller."

"And where's that bitch? Still on the run?"

"Not exactly. She ran right into the arms of the Russians."

"The Russians?" the sidekick said, sounding just as surprised as Chris was. Hairs were standing up on the back of Chris's neck.

"Goddamn right, my friend. She's a traitor who can never return to the USA, so she's claiming asylum. For the Ruskis to have the ex-CIA Director switching sides, it's a Grade A win. The U.S government is gonna be more embarrassed than it has ever been."

"But how does it affect us?"

"She can talk whatever shit she wants to the Russians. If she wants to pin us, she'll have to come back home and testify. Even if she had the spine to face justice, she knows we'd take her out anyway."

"So we're good?"

"We're good."

You, my friends, Chris thought to himself, *are far from good.*

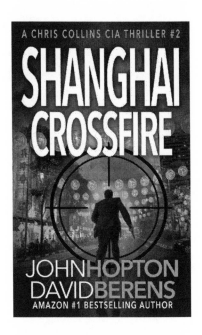

CONTINUE THE ADVENTURE

Could You Betray The Ones You Love For the Greater Good?

Chris Collins is an ex-CIA agent with a history of rogue missions. His enemies took away everything he had, and now it's time to pay. He knows his adversaries will stop at nothing to remove those who stand in their way - including himself. But they move in the shadows, and smoking them out means taking himself to some dark places.

As he hunts them down, he's reminded that for spies like him, romance is never easy. How can you find love when seducing strangers is part of your job description?

Across the world, a child is missing. Will the web finally lead back to him, or will he be lost forever?

This is an action-packed, seductive thriller set across exotic locations.

"A riveting political thriller."
    "Straight out of the Mission Impossible or James Bond films"
    "Fun, fast-paced and intriguing."

Readers of James Rollins, Matthew Reilly, and Mark Dawson will LOVE this series. Pick up a copy, put the phone on silent, and lock the door—this is going to be an all-nighter!

And don't forget to go grab the prequel—ROGUE ENEMY—absolutely free at www.tropicalthrillers.com.

CLICK HERE TO DOWNLOAD YOUR COPY NOW!

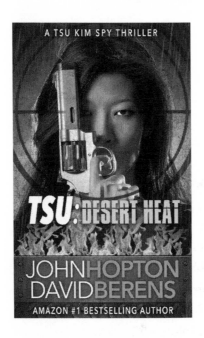

A TSU KIM SPY THRILLER

TSU: DESERT HEAT

JOHN HOPTON
DAVID BERENS

AMAZON #1 BESTSELLING AUTHOR

TSU: DESERT HEAT

The response to the character named Tsu Kim in the Chris Collins thrillers made one thing clear: she needed a story of her own. So, here is her backstory. Fair warning, it's blazing hot!

She's the hottest agent they've got. Maybe she's too hot.

Tsu Kim has finished her espionage training and came out top of her class. From psychometric testing to hand-to-hand combat, she turned heads and made everyone in the agency take note. Now, it's time for the real world.

When a Korean scientist and his daughter are kidnapped in Istanbul, Tsu insists it's a job for her. He superior disagrees. No matter how good she is, she's not ready for this.

So when she finds herself on the streets of the ancient city, everything is on the line, including her reputation and the lives of her compatriots. Will she succeed? And will even her own agency find her too hot to handle?

Readers of James Rollins, Russell Blake, and Matthew Reilly will LOVE this series. Pick up a copy, put the phone on silent, and lock the door—this is going to be an all-nighter!

CLICK HERE TO RESERVE YOUR COPY NOW!

ALSO BY DAVID BERENS

As a thank you for buying this book, I'd like to invite you to join my Beachbum Brigade Reader Group. You can get 4 FREE BOOKS for joining (like some of the prequels mentioned below.)

JOIN HERE: www.tropicalthrillers.com/readergroup if you haven't already.

Troy Bodean Tropical Thrillers

- #0 Tidal Wave (available FREE exclusively to the Beachbum Brigade Reader Group)
- #1 Rogue Wave
- #2 Deep Wave
- #3 Blood Wave
- #4 Dark Wave
- #5 Skull Wave
- #6 Shark Wave
- #7 Gator Wave (COMING SOON)

Jo Bennett Archaeological Mysteries

- #1 Temple of the Snake - With Nick Thacker
- #2 Tomb of the Queen - Nick Thacker & Kristi Belcamino

Ryan Bodean Tropical Thrillers

With Steven Moore

- #0 Havana Fury (available FREE exclusively to the Beachbum Brigade Reader Group)
- #1 Atlantis Storm
- #2 Hemingway Found
- #3 ElDorado Gold

The Prosperity Spartanburg Files

With Cherie Mitchell

- #0 Finding Prosperity (available FREE exclusively to the Beachbum Brigade Reader Group)
- #1 Raising Prosperity
- #2 Prosperity Dawning
- #3 Prosperity Soaring

The Caparelli Family Series

With Cherie Mitchell

- #0 A Hitman for Christmas (bonus Christmas story.)
- #0.5 A Glimpse of a Hitman (available FREE exclusively to the Beachbum Brigade Reader Group)
- #1 The Heart of a Hitman

Chris Collins CIA Thrillers

With John Hopton

- #0 Rogue Enemy (available FREE exclusively to the Beachbum Brigade Reader Group)
- #1 Capitol Break
- #2 Shanghai Crossfire
- #3 To Be Revealed

Tsu Kim Spy Thrillers

With John Hopton

- #0 TSU: Desert Heat

The Southernmost Mystery Series

With Kimberly Griggs

- #0 A Death In The Afternoon (available FREE exclusively to the Beachbum Brigade Reader Group)
- #1 A Farewell To Murder

CAPITOL BREAK

A Chris Collins CIA Thriller
All Rights Reserved © 2020 by David F. Berens

Tropical Thriller Press 2020

Printed in The United States of America

Contact the Author at:
www.TropicalThrillers.com

Made in the USA
Middletown, DE
10 April 2020